"I may not be an obstetrician, but I can count nine months!"

Alex lassoed her with his steady gaze. "Why can't you just admit the baby's mine?"

If she could've gotten up from the rocking chair, she'd have stormed off in a graceful huff, but she left "graceful" behind months ago. "It's just like you to show up and wheedle your way into my good graces," she said instead. "What surprises me is how eager you are to take on a responsibility that belongs to someone else."

"Nice try." He looked confident, sure of himself, altogether too handsome for his own good. Or hers. "I know you wouldn't have come from another man's arms to mine, Annie. And you wouldn't have left me for someone else. *We* made this baby and *I'm* trying to do right by it." His expression sobered, and if she hadn't known better, she'd've thought he looked a bit stunned. "There's only one thing to do," he said. "We'll need to get married."

Dear Reader,

When our editors asked us to write stories about three brothers who wind up in the delivery room near midnight, December 31, 1999, we sat down to think. Good-looking men, pregnant ladies with brains and beauty, and a first baby of the millennium contest—how could we resist?

The friendship we formed as we created DELIVERY ROOM DADS was an added bonus. E-mails flew fast and furious, and when the dust settled, we had a town, a family, a contest and happily-ever-after for everyone involved.

Welcome to Bison City, Wyoming, home of the devastating McIntyre brothers. The baby race begins in Karen Toller Whittenburg's *Baby by Midnight?,* complications arise in Muriel Jensen's *Countdown to Baby* and the winner is revealed at the stroke of midnight in Judy Christenberry's *Baby 2000.* Our characters remind us of the love and strength of family. We hope they do the same for you, too. Thank you for joining us in the delivery room as these special dads ring in the new millennium!

Karen Toller Whittenburg
Muriel Jensen
Judy Christenberry

Baby by Midnight?

KAREN TOLLER WHITTENBURG

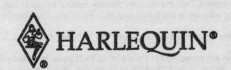

HARLEQUIN®

TORONTO • NEW YORK • LONDON
AMSTERDAM • PARIS • SYDNEY • HAMBURG
STOCKHOLM • ATHENS • TOKYO • MILAN • MADRID
PRAGUE • WARSAW • BUDAPEST • AUCKLAND

ISBN 0-373-16794-6

BABY BY MIDNIGHT?

Copyright © 1999 by Karen Toller Whittenburg.

Visit us at www.romance.net

Printed in U.S.A.

FIRST BABY OF BISON CITY 2000

IT'S A BABY BOOM IN BISON CITY, WYOMING—
BUT WHICH WILL BE THE FIRST BABY BORN IN
THE NEW MILLENNIUM?

ALL YOU PREGNANT WOMEN: ENTER TO WIN!

FABULOUS PRIZES!!
YOUR PHOTO IN THE *BISON CITY BUGLE!!*
A TOWN PARTY IN YOUR HONOR!!

PICK UP YOUR APPLICATION AT ALL LOCAL
BUSINESSES—AND MAY THE FIRST BABY WIN!

To Judy and Muriel, my series partners, for making the journey to Bison City so enjoyable.

And to Natashya, Debra, Denise, Angela and Erica— sometimes editors have the best ideas!

Prologue

The wedding reception had turned plain sappy as far as Alex McIntyre was concerned. Anyone would think his little sister had married a monkey and the whole town of Bison City, Wyoming, was too damn polite to point it out to her. So far, congratulatory toasts to the happy couple had ranged from Reverend Whitehead's heartfelt, "God Bless," to oldest brother, Matt's, story about the time he caught Josie sneaking out of the house after hours. Alex had caught her a few times, too— and let her go. He'd even driven her into town once or twice. But to say so now, even after all the intervening years, would only serve to confirm the general consensus that he wasn't much like his two older brothers. It wouldn't do much to liven up this party, either. Even Jeff, the middle McIntyre brother, had offered little more than the lackluster toast of "May you be blessed with happiness and long life." All that was needed to put the last schmaltzy touch on the evening would be for Sheriff Hitchcock to lead the guests in a resounding chorus of "Happy Trails to You."

For a family as basically rowdy as theirs, Alex thought this whole three-forked, two-spooned, crystal-gobleted dinner was downright embarrassing. He didn't think the formal reception had been Josie's idea. Probably not Justin's, either. Alex suspected his mother was the driving force behind this elaborate wedding and ill-conceived sit-down dinner. A barbecue out at the ranch would have been better suited to this crowd and a hell of a lot more fun, no question about it. But ever since Ken and Debra had turned the ranch over to Matt eight years ago and retired to Florida, they'd picked up some bewildering ideas about ceremonies and civilization.

So, here they all were in the dining room of Jeff's hotel, The Way Station, all duded up in fancy clothes, starched linens in their respective laps, drinking champagne out of glasses so light it was a wonder the bubbles didn't shatter them, and talking in cordial platitudes instead of having a rip-snortin' good time. Matt looked decidedly uncomfortable in his black tie and tails and Alex sure as hell couldn't wait to get out of his. Jeff had more savoir faire, having lived in New York and now being a respectable hotel owner and all. But there was no getting past the fact that McIntyre men were born to be cowboys, more comfortable in their Wrangler jeans and in the company of horses than spiffed up for a wedding.

Yep. No doubt about it. Up near Silver Horn

Lake, in the family cemetery plot, Old Samuel and Jocasta, the great-grandparents of this whole McIntyre clan, had to be yawning in their graves, probably wondering why there was no fiddle music and not a single toe a tappin' on their great-granddaughter's big day.

Something had to be done…and quickly. Alex looked around, figuring that, as usual, the responsibility for shaking up the status quo was his. Pushing back his chair, he gave his best cowboy whoop as he rolled to his feet and raised his beer bottle—he'd never much cottoned to champagne—high above his head. "My baby sister just got married and I'm gonna make a toast!" Heads turned in his direction, frowns descended on a few faces, but Josie and Justin looked up with hopeful smiles. They must have been as bored as he was.

Alex winked at Jo, a little melancholy at the thought of her living clear across town, at the idea that she'd no longer fly down the porch steps to hug his neck on the rare occasions when he came back to the ranch for a visit, loving her mightily despite the fact that she'd agreed to this formal-schmormal reception. "When Josie told me she was going into politics some day, it certainly didn't occur to me she was going to wind up sleeping with the mayor." There was a general chuckle, one outright grin from Justin, and continued interest from most everybody else. "Now, I could be wrong about this," Alex continued, "but I'm figurin' that somewhere along the way Dad must've made a whoppin' contribution to Justin's reelection campaign." This brought good-natured laughter all around, as it was well known that until Justin Moore followed Josie McIntyre home from the University of Wyoming, Bison City hadn't even had a mayor, much less a contested election for the post. "My brothers and I have talked about this and, while it's a mystery to us why any man would willingly share a bathroom with Josie, we want you to know, Justin, that you get our vote for bravery. Plus you're gonna have to keep her, 'cause we're not taking her back."

"That's for sure." Matt raised his glass and clinked it against Jeff's. "Besides, it took her long enough to decide to marry you. Good thing the men in this family don't have that much trouble making up their minds."

"As if any woman in her right mind would have one of you big bullies." Josie stuck out her tongue at their teasing, and dimpled becomingly at her husband of a few hours.

Justin leaned over and kissed his bride, then raised his glass. "I'm just happy I came along before she followed Alex's example and went off to 'find' herself."

Alex drank to that. It was true he'd spent most of his twenty-nine years doing his damnedest to locate his niche in the world. Or maybe he'd just been trying to escape the responsibilities of being born a McIntyre. Either way, he'd done some wild and stupid things in pursuit of the goal. In fact, if he announced right now that he was planning to move back, set up as a horse trainer and start a pedigreed breeding program at the ranch, well, not one person in the room would believe he meant it.

Least of all Annie.

In the back of the room, he saw her drink to the haphazard toast, her hair glinting red in the soft light. He actually thought about walking across the tops of the tables to reach her, thought about how weak in the knees he got every time he caught that first breath-snatching glimpse of her smile. He'd like nothing better than to sweep her into his arms and demonstrate that he was one McIntyre who didn't have any trouble making up his mind.

But then what?

Goodbye, that's what. That was the deal he'd made with the devil. Alex was always leaving, and Annie was always staying behind. It was the way it had always been for them. The way it still had to be.

"Despite all evidence to the contrary," Alex said, returning his attention to the head table, to Josie and her bridegroom. "I'm plum tickled to be here today to wish my favorite sister—"

"Your *only* sister," someone called out in well-meaning good humor.

"My *only* sister," Alex agreed with a grin. "As most everyone here is aware, tradition isn't exactly my cup of coffee, but today I'm awed by the courage of Josie and Justin to say those marriage vows…and mean them."

"They'd better mean 'em," Ken McIntyre grumbled cheerfully. "This wedding darn sure cost too much for anybody to be wishy-washy about it lasting till death do 'em part.''

"As I was sayin','' Alex continued, pointedly. "I'm inspired by my sister and her fella and I hope, someday, that you'll all dance at my... *brothers'* weddings.'' Laughter echoed about the room, everyone in on the joke that Alex wasn't the marrying kind. When the ripples of sound ebbed, he lifted his beer one more time. "So, Josie and Justin, here's to you. Long life, long nights, and don't be in any big hurry to make me an uncle. I'm too set in my ways for that kind of responsibility. Now will you *please* get up and start the dancin' before everybody's feet fall asleep?''

Amid laughter and applause, the bride and groom got up from the table and made their way to the open space reserved as a dance floor. Jasper's No-Name Band struck the first notes of "The Wild West Waltz," and the party took an immediate right turn for the better. Alex's toe had just started tapping when a hand grabbed his arm and he turned to see Wilhemina Brown, minus her usual 'Cause I'm the Cook! That's Why! apron, her pink cheeks rosy with celebration. "Hold on there, mister," she said. "Don't you even think about grabbin' some frisky little filly when I'm standin' not two feet away.''

"Willie! I was looking all over for you.'' Alex smiled broadly at the McIntyres' housekeeper and all-around care giver. "You know I always save the first dance for you.''

"Humph. I know you always dance the first

dance with the cutest thing you can get your hands on,'' she said in her best fist-of-iron, heart-of-jelly voice. ''But I used to change your diapers, and if I say we're gonna dance, then don't you give me no sass.'' Her blue eyes twinkled with long familiarity and genuine adoration. The McIntyre children were her kids, even if they weren't blood relations, and she'd fight anyone who claimed any different. ''Now, you gonna lead or you want me to?''

''I'll lead. Otherwise you'll be twirling me all over the place and making me plum dizzy.'' Alex swept her into the dance, corralling her plump waist with one arm and holding on for dear life with the other as she loped into a brisk one-two-three waltz step. She then proceeded to bombard him with advice about what he ate, how much sleep he got, and her worry that he wasn't taking good care of himself. It felt good to be fussed over, and at times like this Alex wondered why he'd ever left the S-J Ranch and the familiar relationships of home. Then Matt tapped him on the shoulder, danced Willie right out of his arms, and he remembered. Here in Bison City, he was just the youngest of three brothers. All tall, all dark and blue-eyed, all sharing the same upbringing and values. All alike in so many fundamental ways. All different in so many others. Here he was Alex, the wild one. Alex, the irresponsible. Alex, the prodigal son.

He glanced back at the table where Annie had been sitting and saw an empty chair. His heart beat faster, afraid she'd left early, taking with her his hope that there might—just might—be an opportunity to dance with her. Providing, of course, that she was still speaking to him after their last, acrimonious goodbye. He wouldn't blame her if she couldn't bear to be in the same building with him, but a fast visual sweep of the room found her dancing with Jeff, her head tipped back as she talked to him, her coppery hair curling in springy tendrils about her shoulders, the sway of her hips defined by the fit of a slim, green dress.

Relief caught him like a summer shower and revived the hope. Not that he had any business going near her and starting something he couldn't finish. He was leaving again—in the morning, right after he sat down with Matt and Jeff and laid out his plans. If his brothers backed him up on the idea, he'd be coming home for good in the fall. If everything worked out the way he hoped, he'd be back in Annie's good graces by New Year's Day. Christmas, if he was lucky. If he told her that now, though, she'd never believe him. Heaven knew, she always assumed the worst with him...not that there wasn't plenty of worst to assume. He'd spent most of his life not living up to expectations, thinking that was the way to keep from disappointing. Maybe he'd been wrong to be so careless with Annie. On the other hand, maybe he'd spared them both a lot of heartache.

Not that she'd ever let him get within breaking distance of her heart.

Nor was she likely to, either. It'd be better all around if he just stayed away from her until he had something more than another goodbye to offer. It'd be harder, sure, but it wasn't as if he'd ever taken the easy way, no matter what the circumstances. Straightening his shoulders, Alex turned around and asked the first woman he saw to dance. She was one of the bridesmaids, Bailey Dutton, and her diminutive, softly curved body fit warmly into his embrace. She was smart, cute, witty, and laughed at his jokes, and Alex settled in to enjoy a second dance. But Jasper Owens, lead singer of Jasper's No-Name Band, had other ideas. Grabbing the microphone, which squawked like a mule at feeding time, Jasper pulled it up too close to his lips. Alex half expected the man to yell out, "Live from Bison City...it's Saturday Night!"

"Okay, you party animals." Jasper popped the consonants into the mike and sent reverberations booming across the room. "Mix it up out there. Change partners for this next one. It's a little song me and the boys wrote. We call it the 'Goodbye-Baby Two-Step!'" The music changed, picked up tempo. Couples swapped partners, and before he even saw it coming, Alex was handing Bailey over to Jeff and taking Annie's hand in exchange.

Good intentions fled like a coyote from a fight. Noble as the gesture might be, he couldn't just walk away and leave her standing alone on the dance floor. She could have slapped his face for past offenses, told him she'd rather dance with Fred Astaire's evil twin and walked away from him, without a soul in the room thinking it was any less than he deserved. But she wouldn't do that. Alex knew she wouldn't. And he couldn't leave her there. So he drew her into the dance and, although he was almost positive he'd live to regret this moment, he was one happy cowboy just to be holding Annie in his arms.

"Hello, Annie," he said.

"Hello, cowboy," she answered, as if he were nobody special.

"Ah, you recognized me." He matched her tone for tone. "And I thought this was such a great disguise, too."

Her smile was brief. "You forget, I've seen you in a tux before."

And there it was. *Plop.* Like a bad penny. Past crimes and misdemeanors. "I could do the grovel," he suggested, "but we'd be out of step with the music."

She lifted her lashes and nailed him with her green-eyed gaze. "I thought that's the way you preferred to dance, Alex."

Okay. So maybe it would be next Easter before he talked her around. "I prefer to enjoy the moment and the melody," he said diplomatically, just as Jasper and his No-Name Band launched into an ill-timed chorus, consisting mainly of the lyrics, "Goodbye, baby, goodbye."

Annie smiled. "Well, what do you know? They're playing your song."

Alex clinched his jaw, took a deep breath and unclinched it. "How 'bout we go back and start this conversation over? I'll go first. Hi, Annie. You look beautiful."

"Do you think so?" She cocked her pretty head and whapped him with a smile. "You should see me when I go to a lot of trouble to fix myself up."

Oh, no, he thought. Is the Statute of Limitations *ever* going to run out on this one? "You always look terrific," he said, hoping to head her off at the pass.

No such luck. "But on certain occasions," she said with a saucy toss of her head, "I really outdo myself. I buy an expensive dress, matching shoes, get my hair done, a manicure, all the time thinking I'm actually going to go to a real nice party with a real nice guy."

"Ah, see, there's your problem. I've been telling you for years to stay away from those nice guys." Alex pulled her a bit closer...so if she took an actual swing at him, she wouldn't have room to pack much wallop behind it. "You just can't depend on them."

"I keep forgetting it's you bad boys I should be counting on."

"Bad? Why, Miss Thatcher, you have cut me to the quick. All this time I thought you understood I was one of the good guys."

"Oh, that's right," she said in that sweet-as-butter tone. "It wasn't like you intended to stand me up. It was just circumstances beyond your control that prevented you from showing up...or calling...or even sending a note after the fact."

"Inexcusable, I know, but on that particular occasion, the, uh, circumstances were pretty compelling. And the minute I got back into town, I did put on a tux, rent a limo and show up at your door with flowers, souvenirs, my profuse apologies and a sincere explanation. All of which, I might remind you, you did eventually accept.''

''Yes.'' Her voice softened with the memory, then sharpened. ''But it still doesn't make up for the fact that I had to go stag to my own twenty-fifth birthday party.''

Alex wanted to run a finger under his collar to loosen it a bit, but he grinned down at her instead. ''And just to make up for that, I've missed every single one of your birthday parties since. See, I am a thoughtful guy.''

She looked at him for a moment as they danced. ''You're trouble to the core, McIntyre,'' she said. ''Which makes me an idiot for being happy to see you.''

Okay, so the incident was never going to be forgotten. At least she'd forgiven him…and he owed her for that. ''Don't kid me, kiddo. Admit it. You're just happy to see me trussed up in this cummerbund and bow tie.''

''Well,'' she said. ''There is something to be said for a man in a tuxedo.''

''Yes, there is, but you probably shouldn't say it in mixed company.''

Her soft laugh was as refreshing as a cold beer on a hot day. ''How long are you staying this time, Alex?''

''Not long.''

''That part I already knew.''

He wished he could give her another answer or

that he could ask her to go with him. But their timing was always off. That's just the way their Kismet worked. "I'm leaving tomorrow. Going back to Texas."

She nodded. "I've heard it gets real hot there in the summer."

"So they tell me. I'll send you a postcard when the temperature hits a hundred." He paused. "Same address?"

"As if I could afford to move out of Uncle Dex's house. I'll be paying for this veterinary degree until I die."

"Hey, that's right. I'm supposed to address you as Dr. Thatcher, now, aren't I?" Another mistake. He realized it the minute the words left his mouth.

His dismay must have shown on his face because she simply shook her head. "Oh, don't look so stricken," she said. "I'd probably have had a heart attack if you had shown up at my graduation."

"I wanted to be there, Annie. I meant to surprise you, but I had the chance to fill in for one of the trainers and—"

"And you seized the opportunity with both hands and your whole heart. I know how this works, Alex, and believe me, I'm not angry. I stopped expecting you to show up for the major events in my life a long time ago."

He thought that was a little unfair. "You have to admit I've been there for some pretty important moments."

The music stopped as she lifted solemn eyes to

his. "Yes, Alex, sometimes, you have been the only one I could count on."

Impulsively, gently, his fingers brushed the soft curve of her neck. History, he thought. They had it in spades...and more good than bad, no matter what she believed at the moment. Suddenly it was on the tip of his tongue to tell her everything, to pour out the plans he was making, the success waiting at the end of his carefully constructed rainbow. "Annie, I'm coming back...in the fall...and then we—"

"Don't." She cut him off...and he heard the echo of past goodbyes in her voice. "You've never made me any promises, Alex. Don't ruin your spotless record now."

For a moment the future hung there between them, like a drifter who'd run out of places to go. She looked at him, questioning. He looked at her with the answer...and then he felt a tap on his shoulder.

"Hey, little brother," Matt said with a grin, as he edged Alex out. "You're too ugly to dance with Annie. Move aside."

Jasper's "Saturday Night Live" voice geared down to a Harry Connick, Jr., croon, and a soft, romantic ballad drew lovers together across the room.

"Not tonight," Alex told Matt, refusing to relinquish his claim. "I may be ugly, but I'm not as ugly as you. And either way, Annie would still rather dance with me." Then he swept her away, willing to let the moment and the melody lead them where it would.

No pretense. No plans. No promises. Nothing except the hours between midnight, morning and one last bittersweet goodbye.

Chapter One

"Don't do it, mutt." Alex put his foot on the brake the minute he caught sight of the shepherd-collie mix at the side of the road up ahead. The dog looked dirty, disheveled and desperate...and not necessarily in that order. It just stood there, staring across the highway, not moving, but somehow obviously contemplating the crossing. Even from this distance, it was clear to Alex that the dog didn't particularly care whether he made it to the other side. "Don't do it," Alex repeated, applying more pressure to the brake.

As the old pickup slowed, the motor sputtered and grabbed, choked down, then miraculously caught again and chugged on. Alex knew he was lucky the truck had made it this far without breaking down. The heavy horse trailer would have been a drag on the engine even if the truck wasn't due a major overhaul and Lord only knew how many replacement parts. But it was more important that the horse travel in comfort, and after he'd spent so much money on the trailer, the '80 model GMC was the best Alex could afford to pull it. Matt and Jeff would laugh themselves into next month when they laid eyes on the old pickup, but Alex figured they needed to know he could cut corners as well as anybody when he had to.

Besides, they'd quit laughing when they saw the horse.

Fifty miles more and he'd be in Bison City. Home, for the first time in six months. Home to stay...and that was a first, too. Once he got there, the truck could die for all he cared. He just needed it to hold out for those last few miles, that's all. Just ahead, the dog shook itself and took a couple of stiff-jointed steps onto the road, directly in front of the truck. Alex laid on the horn, and the dog jerked back, suddenly aware of the danger and trembling visibly. Or maybe Alex just had an over-active imagination when it came to animals. Either way, the noise seemed to pay off, because the dog retreated from the roadway and was standing several feet back when Alex drove past and lost sight of him. "It's a good day to go home," he said, offering a word of advice to the dog...or anyone who happened to be listening.

It was a glorious October day, all sun and sky and crisp autumn air, and it didn't get much better than driving home on a long road with one elbow out the open window and one hand loosely guiding the steering wheel. He'd just pursed his lips to whistle "Home on the Range" when his pickup crested a small incline and met another vehicle, which flew past like a cat with its tail on fire. He heard the blast of a car horn, a screech of brakes, then the accelerating whine of the engine as the car resumed speed and roared on. Suddenly Alex imagined a whole other unpleasant scenario—the shepherd-collie lying crushed and suffering as the hit-and-run speeder flew on to parts unknown.

"Dang it," Alex said aloud, pulling onto the shoulder where he stopped the truck and killed the engine. It'd be a miracle if the motor cranked up again...and all because he was a soft touch and had to go back to check on a dumb dog. Fifty miles, he thought. Give or take a couple. And he would walk every last one of them rather than call one of his brothers and ask to be fetched the rest of the way home.

Both Jeff and Matt were going to be real put out with him as it was, and he saw no need to let them get a head start on the dressing down he expected they were gonna give him. He'd talk them around, though. Sooner or later. Once he got them to take a good look at Koby, they'd understand bloodlines weren't the only thing that counted in a good cutting horse. Once his brothers got used to the idea, they'd realize Alex did know his way around a training arena and that he was no greenhorn when it came to picking a winner.

Right now, though, he had to see about a dumb dog. Getting out of the pickup, he slammed the door and had to hit it twice with the flat of his hand to close it completely. He walked past the faded blue truck bed and the sleek new Silver-Stream horse trailer, stopping once to stick his hand through the open window and give Koby a reassuring pat. The quarter horse snuffled restlessly, and Alex headed on up the incline, hoping hard that the dog would be long gone by the time he reached the top. Even though there wasn't a house within miles. Even though there wasn't much of anything except grazing land and plains rolling off toward the Bighorn Mountains. Dumb dog. Why couldn't he have stayed home where he belonged?

As Alex crested the hill, he took a deep breath, then let it out in relief when he saw the dog—still among the living—lying on his stomach beside the road, his head bent as he licked furiously at his front paw. Maybe the car had missed him altogether. Maybe he'd just picked up a sticker burr. Or had decided it was time to wash up. But as Alex approached, he saw skid marks and the drops of blood that led to where the collie now lay. "Ah, hell," he said under his breath and moved closer to the animal.

"Hi-ya, fella." Sinking onto his heels, Alex observed the dog from a reasonable distance. He didn't want to get bitten and have to spend the rest of the afternoon at the small Bison City Hospital waiting for old Doc Wilson to wander in and give him a tetanus shot. "How bad is it?" he asked, running a calculating eye over the animal, deciding he was more collie than shepherd, more alive than dead—although that was purely a judgment call. The dog kept licking at the paw, but his eyes followed Alex with fear and pain and just a touch of melancholy hope.

"Mind if I take a look at that? I'll do my best not to hurt you." Alex scooted forward, careful to move slowly and to keep soothing the dog with the sound of his voice. "You can't stay here, y'know. Road like this is a dangerous spot for a guy like you. Not enough traffic to keep you on your toes. What are you doing out here, anyway? It's gettin' on toward supper time, y'know. Time to be headin' home."

When the dog offered no challenge, Alex put out a hand and stroked the matted fur at his neck. He didn't touch the leg. He didn't have to. At closer range, it was easy to see the animal wasn't going to shake off this injury and trot on home. The bleeding seemed to be coming from a superficial cut, but there could be internal injuries as well, and he was fairly certain the left front leg was broken. Add to that the fact the dog was as skinny as a toothless coyote, lost in the middle of nowhere, and looked for all the world like he was too depressed to care.

Alex stroked the collie's head and felt him sigh beneath the gentle comfort. Then his fingers scraped across a worn leather collar buried beneath the fur, and there was the brief, unmistakable jingle of vaccination tags. This guy belonged to somebody. "All right, fella," he said, carefully turning the collar until he could see the wording on the tags. The vaccination was current and listed a Sheridan veterinary clinic. "You've traveled a piece, haven't you?" Either that, or someone had dumped him. Sad to say, there were still people that stupid. With a shake of his head, Alex got ready to scoop the dog into his arms and carry him back to the truck. "I know this isn't going to be real pleasant for you," he said, "but bear with me and don't bite. You may find this hard to believe, mutt, but your luck just changed for the better."

ANNIE HAD HER HANDS FULL of frantic cat.

"I never thought about him going in the laundry room there." Hilda Lawson worked her hands like a wringer washing machine. "Why, those spider traps hadn't been set out twenty minutes before I heard him yowl. You think you can get those off him?"

"Not without giving him a crew cut. Genevieve!" Annie yelled again for her assistant as she tried to keep the Lawsons' massive tomcat from leaping off the examining table and climbing the wallpapered wall.

"Now, Samson," Hilda scolded gently, all the while keeping a cautious distance from the scrambling mass of yellow fur and sharp claws. "You be still for Dr. Annie. She just wants to get those nasty sticky strips off you."

Actually, what Annie wanted was to get Genevieve in here to help so she could put this muleheaded tom in a cage until he calmed down. As it stood, her hands and arms were already stinging from cat scratches, and it was all she could do to keep him on the table.

Samson was a prize fighter of a feline. Easily the heavyweight champ of all Bison City's cats— with myriad battle scars to prove it. One ear was missing a chunk of flesh, and the other dipped toward his eye like a low-riding hat. His tail had a kink, he walked with a limp, and he had a chronic case of bad attitude. He hated the veterinary clinic and everyone in it. Annie wasn't sure he really liked Hilda, but he was her baby and occasionally he allowed her to treat him like the petite pedigreed Persian she seemed to believe he was.

At least, Hilda claimed he loved her. Annie hadn't seen any sign the cat would know affection from affliction—and she'd seen Samson on a fairly regular basis ever since June when she'd taken over most of the doctoring from her Uncle Dex. She'd treated the old cat for everything from constipation to snake bite and privately thought he had to be long into his ninth and last life. Today he'd tangled with several long strips of adhesive meant to trap spiders and other crawling insects. He was glued paw to ear and fur to fur, and this time Annie thought he might just have met his match.

"Genevieve!" She yelled again and tried to hold the cat, dab the glue strips with rubbing alcohol, and snip at the cat's fur all at the same time. He broke free suddenly and leaped for the counter, where his three-legged scrambling scattered containers of cotton swabs and doggie treats. He sprang for the stainless steel sink and landed short, his claws frantically grabbing for a hold as he slid down the front of the cabinet.

"I got him!" Hilda yelled, although she made only a lame attempt to grab him. Her voice had an invigorating effect on Samson, though. He made a clumsy dive under the examining table and came out the other side, with an Ace wrap adhered to one of the glue strips still adhered to him. The bandage unrolled and trailed out behind him, like a long, ecru shadow, scaring him anew and sending him dashing around the table, then around the other side. At this rate he was going to either hang himself or wind up as a cat mummy. Which wouldn't make a good reference for the doc who'd treated him.

Annie sighed and got down on her knees, holding on to the examining table to offset the imbalance of her protruding tummy. Dr. Elizabeth had warned her that work was going to get increasingly difficult as the pregnancy progressed, but moments like this one at least took Annie's mind off her worries. And really, what was worse?—being an unmarried mom-to-be or being a cat who was about to lose a whole lot of hair? Maybe even a little hide, if he wasn't caught soon.

Calculating the avenues for escape, Annie stalked Samson on her hands and knees and almost had him cornered by the door when Genevieve decided—with her usual dramatic timing—that she was needed in Examining Room One. She opened the door, and in a split second Samson spied the light of freedom, sensed salvation and made a mad dash between the newcomer's hefty ankles. Annie had mere nanoseconds to make a decision and,

with the faint comfort that Samson could handle
most any patient awaiting him in the waiting room,
she cut the trailing bandage to a less-cumbersome
length and let him go.

"What in Sweet Pete is going on in here?" Genevieve demanded, hands braced on hips that had
borne eight children and still carried a few pounds
from each as a souvenir. Her stern gaze swept from
the hand-wringing Hilda to the floor where Annie,
still on all fours, looked up at her with sincere
frustration. "What? You couldn't wait a minute for
me to get in here and help you?"

It was an ongoing battle between them. Genevieve had assisted Dexter Thatcher for forty-two
years and figured she'd earned her degree in the
school of experience. She didn't trust anyone—
namely Annie—who'd graduated college in the
last decade to handle the paying customers, which
Samson wasn't, but Hilda definitely was. Since
taking over at the clinic, Annie had done everything she could think of to establish her role as the
doctor in charge. To date Genevieve remained un-
impressed. She knew Annie couldn't afford to fire
her, and she knew she wasn't about to quit. So here
they were once again. Stalemate.

"Could you go get Samson before he does some
serious damage?" Annie grabbed hold of the table
and pulled herself upright. From the waiting room
came the sound of the collar-and-leash display top-
pling, a cat's *meowwwlll,* a terrier's startled *yap,*
the chime of the front door opening and closing,

the deep vibrations of a male voice asking to see Dr. Thatcher. And it was only Monday.

"I'll fetch him." Genevieve turned in the doorway, not hurrying—never that—just eyeing the hallway before her and the archway into the waiting room beyond. "What in tarnation did you let that yellow son of Sam get into this time, Hilda?"

"Pest strips," Hilda answered, worrying along behind Genevieve. "We've had a rash of spiders this fall, and Pete thought it'd be a good idea to put out traps, but I never thought about Samson gettin' stuck on 'em."

"Curiosity's gonna kill that cat one of these days," Genevieve pronounced as she plodded toward what sounded like a terrier and tomcat battleground. "And there ain't gonna be 'nough satisfaction out there to bring him back."

Annie sighed and leaned against the table. She knew she was lucky beyond belief that Uncle Dex wanted her to run his clinic. She knew she was lucky to have his long experience behind her when she needed it. She knew she was lucky to be practicing her calling in Bison City, where she had the support of friends and long acquaintances. But there were moments—this one a prime example— when she wished she hadn't been so lucky as to inherit Genevieve.

"Get that cat out of my way, Hilda!" Genevieve bellowed suddenly. "Bring him on back here, Alex. Examining Room One." She bustled into the room again like a drum major leading the parade, all pomp and circumstance.

Annie straightened. Alex? "What is it?" she asked, even as she tried to see around Genevieve's efficient preparations to swipe the table with an antiseptic cloth. Then Alex was in the room, his dark hair disheveled, his blue eyes troubled, his strong arms burdened with dog. Injured dog. Annie took in the situation in a glance and, despite feeling as jumpy as a cat trapped in a room full of no-pest strips, she moved into action. "Put him on the table. What happened?"

Alex hesitated, then laid the dog on the metal table and stepped back. "Hit," he said in a strange voice. "Car. Speeding. About fifty miles out."

Annie heard the nuance in his voice, recognized that he was tense, distressed, upset, but her energy and skill was centered on the dog. She had to stay focused. There was no time now to worry about Alex. Or to wonder what he was doing here. Or to think about the last time he was home. No, she especially couldn't afford to think about that. "How fast were you going?" She snapped off the question as her hands moved over the dog, checking vital signs, assessing the damage, calculating what needed to be done.

"I don't know. Sixty, maybe. I slowed down when I saw him."

"Her. It's a female," Annie corrected, wishing Alex wasn't always speeding through life, slowing down only when he noticed he'd hurt something…or someone. "But you still hit her."

"Yes," he said, then, "No. No, I didn't hit him—her. Look, could I talk to you a minute?"

She looked up, met his eyes, felt the jolt of awareness all the way to her toes...and these days it was a long way down there. "We have nothing to talk about except how this animal came to be injured."

"You're pregnant." His voice was soft, hopeful, scared.

"Yes. And you're in the way. Genevieve? I'm going to need a set of X-rays of this leg. I think she just had a glancing blow to that leg, but let's test for internal bleeding."

For once Genevieve did as she was told. She might be obstinate when it came to giving Samson a much-needed haircut, but she knew when to turn over the responsibility to someone else. This dog might have serious problems, might not make it...and Genevieve's heart couldn't bear to have any part in that. Annie glanced up at Alex, who was still in the room, still staring at her, his gaze roaming from her face to the rounded shape of her belly beneath the cat-and-dog-patterned fabric of her maternity smock. "Alex?" She waved him toward the door. "Would you go on out to the waiting room and see if you can calm Hilda down? You might tell Dinah—she's the cute blonde at the front desk—to put the terrier in the other exam room or else try to get Samson into a cage." He made no move to leave the room, and Annie tried again. "There's nothing you can do in here, Alex. Nothing you even need to worry about. I'll let you know how this little lady's doing as soon as I know."

"You're pregnant," he repeated, obviously stunned by the thought, by the fact of it.

And it was a fact. She was pregnant...and she'd known he'd have to find out about it sometime. Just not now. Not before the baby was born. Not until she had more time to prepare her story and strengthen her resolve that this time Alex wasn't going to talk his way back into her life. This time she had someone else to consider. "Do me a favor, Alex," she said firmly. "Go away. I am perfectly capable of handling this situation on my own."

He held her gaze—blue eyes locked with green—and the question filled the space between them for what seemed like forever before he finally gave it a form. "Mine?"

She wasn't ready for this. Not here. Not now. Not in front of Genevieve. "No," she said, turning her attention back to the dog, burying her hands in the soft, dirty fur so that Alex couldn't see how violently they trembled. "It's mine."

ALEX PACED THE WAITING ROOM like an expectant— Oh, jeez. He didn't want even to think the word. But there it was, nipping his heels like a flea-bitten pup. Distracting, distressing, and wondrously possible. *Father. Father. Father.* Annie was pregnant. She was going to have a baby. His baby? Of course, his. It had to be. Who else would she have—

The idea of Annie with another man wasn't anything he was prepared to consider. She'd loved him since eighth grade when he'd told Jason Kettridge to quit harassing her. Jason hadn't taken kindly to the advice and invited Alex to discuss it after class. In retrospect Alex supposed that the fact they both were suspended from school for a week for fighting probably did more to convince Jason he was in the wrong than any punch Alex might have landed. But the bottom line was Annie—and from the moment he'd challenged her antagonist, she looked at Alex with new eyes. She'd never had anyone much to stand up for her, and while Alex wasn't exactly the ideal knight in shining armor, she didn't seem to mind. Over the years he'd done his best to convince her he didn't deserve her devotion, that she could do lots better than him, but the idea that she might have fallen in love with someone else simply wasn't acceptable.

Plus, the timing was all wrong for that possibility. Not that he was an obstetrician, but he hadn't exactly flunked biology, either, and from what he could tell by looking, Annie was about six months along. Which put the conception back to April, which would line up with Josie's wedding, which would line up with the night he and Annie had danced at the wedding reception, which meant his theory was possible. Probable, even, considering that dancing wasn't all they'd shared that night.

Alex paced some more and forced himself to think about other possibilities. Unpleasant ones, like the idea that she might be more than six months pregnant, in which case he couldn't be the father. Or less than six months, which would also rule him out. Was he being just plain arrogant to think he was the only man she'd ever slept with? And that with only the one night of sweet communion, he'd managed to make her pregnant? That wasn't just arrogant. It was a flat-out jump to conclusions, like a man who finds a shiny rock and goes right out and buys a Cadillac on the theory he's discovered a gold mine.

But no matter how he tossed the possibilities, he kept coming back to the one that made him the father of her baby. It seemed, somehow, easier to deal with the sudden, surprising discovery that he was going to become a father than to face the possibility of Annie being pregnant with another man's child. And it wasn't like he wanted to be well on his way to becoming a father. Alex wasn't sure he'd know what to do with a baby. It certainly wasn't part of his plans for the next year. The next several years for that matter. At the end of December, at the Midwestern Cutting Horse Futurity, he had his first real opportunity to prove to his brothers that he wasn't some ne'er-do-well, but a McIntyre through and through. Once Koby swept the prizes in the cutting division, Alex would be the most sought-after horse trainer in the country. With that one win, the breeding program at the S-J would jump from a minor part of the ranch operations to a viable money-maker.

Alex had planned for this opportunity a lot of years. He had things to prove to a whole bunch of people, but mostly he had to prove to himself that he could follow a dream through to the end of its rainbow and pat himself on the back for the accomplishment, no matter how it turned out. He wanted to stand shoulder to shoulder with Matt and Jeff, to finally feel as if he'd earned their respect, man to man. Annie being pregnant wasn't exactly the way he'd hoped to begin the process, that was for sure.

It wasn't the way he'd meant to start over with her, either. He'd thought he'd have time to do some proper courting, planned to show her over a period of months that he was home to stay, that he wanted the white picket fence and all the rest that made up the life she'd always, and only, wanted. He'd thought there'd be time to prove to her that beneath his rusty armor beat the heart of a gallant and responsible knight.

But a baby. Someone tiny and helpless and dependent. Someone for whom he'd be responsible. Someone who'd need him wholly. Not just when it was convenient, but every day for the rest of his life. Scary thought, that, even for a knight. A baby. Annie's baby. *His.*

Okay, so he'd adjust. He'd overcome the obstacles. He'd stick with his plans. He'd finish Koby's training, win the cutting futurity in December, garner a standing ovation from his family, *and* become a father. He could do it…easy. Well, it wouldn't exactly be easy, but he could do it. It wasn't as if he hadn't done things the hard way before.

Strange, he thought, that no one had bothered to tell him Annie was pregnant. Josie, who announced to complete strangers that *she'd* gotten pregnant on her wedding night, who had kept him apprised of her own condition from morning sickness to stretch marks, had failed to mention that most interesting piece of information. On the other hand, the omission spoke volumes for his theory that he was the father. Josie would have told him if there was another man in Annie's life. She knew their history, had told Alex times out of mind he was an idiot to treat Annie as if she'd always be there, as if she'd wait forever for him to come home. If Annie had fallen in love with someone else, Josie would have told him. She wouldn't have let him come home without some kind of warning. So, since she hadn't told him anything, the baby must be his.

Had to be his.

Fate wouldn't take Annie away from him just when he'd finally figured life out.

A father.

Alex swallowed hard and paced the clinic floor some more.

HE WAS OUTSIDE, walking a sleek bay stallion back and forth between the clinic and the stables behind it, when Annie came out. She stood at the door for a minute, just looking at him, feeling the familiar longing that crept over her like sunup after a really dark night every single time she laid eyes on this man. Alex McIntyre was wrong for her in more ways than she could count, and for years she had gone out of her way to be foolish over him. But no more. April had been the end of it. She had said her last goodbye to him then...and meant it. Alex was always leaving, was always going to be leaving, and she wasn't going to spend another day waiting for him to drop in—and out—of her life. So she'd set her mind to it and determined to get on with life after Alex. That's when she found out she was pregnant.

Fate, as it turned out, had a warped sense of humor.

Lifting her chin, Annie stepped off the concrete slab that served as the clinic's back porch and walked out to meet Alex as he turned and started back toward her. The horse beside him tossed his dark head and pulled on the lead. Spirited. Annie could tell that by looking. Something about the straight-shouldered bay sparked her memory, too, but she couldn't catch the thought fast enough, and it flitted away, undiscovered. She had not much idea what Alex was doing with the horse. From the trailer parked in the drive, she assumed he was taking the horse to the ranch. Or from the ranch. But she was certain Josie would have warned her if he was in town. On the other hand, Josie probably didn't know he was here. Alex wasn't a great one for letting people know his plans—even if one of the people happened to be his sister.

Josie had to suspect her brother had fathered the child Annie carried. Truth be told, most people in Bison City probably had a fair idea that Alex was the father. But none of them knew for certain, because Annie wasn't telling. And that's the way she meant to keep it, too.

"Flashy-looking horse," she said as she fell into

step with Alex and the bay. "Are you training or just transporting him?"

"All that and more. Meet Koby." Alex patted the horse's neck and offered Annie a slanted smile. "That's short for Kodiak Blue."

The fleeting thought dropped into place like a sledgehammer. She stepped back to give the horse a better look. "Alex McIntyre," she said. "Don't tell me this is that Texas twister of a quarter horse Trevor Hankins was talking about at last year's Quarter Horse Congress?"

Alex winked at her. "You're lookin' at him."

Annie couldn't believe it. Matt would have conniptions if Alex came home with this horse. "You bought him?"

"Lock, stock and barrel."

She rubbed the back of her neck. "You paid actual money for him?"

"A goodly chunk of it, yeah. He's going to win the cutting division of the Midwest Futurity later this year. You can bank on it."

Koby sidestepped restlessly, showing signs of the temperament that had earned him that bad-boy reputation, but Alex settled him down with words so soft Annie couldn't even make them out. "Matt isn't going to be happy," she said, and saw by his expression that Alex was well aware of it.

"Matt's never happy with much of anything I do. Jeff, either. But they'll get over it. In fact, they'll be eating their hats before I'm through. And you can bank on that one, too."

Annie bit her bottom lip, hoping he was right,

hoping this time Alex could turn a losing proposition into a winner. She could see where the challenge would appeal to him, knew he'd always thought he had something to prove to the world. Or to the world of the McIntyres, anyway. But that's not what she and Alex had to discuss. "I think I'll just keep my money in my sock," she said, striving for a light tone. "No banks, no bets…no interest."

Alex's gaze dropped to her stomach, then returned to her face. "You might have told me before now, Annie."

"Told you what?"

"That you're…that we're pregnant."

"*We're* not pregnant. I am." She paused to let that soak into his thick skull. "And even supposing I had some overwhelming reason to inform you—which I didn't—how would I have gone about doing that? Sent a postcard to General Delivery, Somewhere, U.S.A?"

"Josie knows where I've been. We've been on the phone to each other at least once a week these past six months. Lord knows, all she talks about lately is how much weight she's gained and what she's bought for the baby and something about starting some kind of contest. First Baby of Bison City 2000…or something like that. It seems sort of odd she never mentioned the two of you were running neck and neck to win that contest."

"I doubt she thought you'd be interested, Alex," Annie said bravely. "I'm a little surprised myself."

"Like hell you are. That baby's mine. I know it as well as you do."

"Really? How do you know that?"

"Josie's six months along and she got pregnant on her wedding night...and if you're both due at the same time..."

Annie had hoped he wouldn't be quite so quick with the math. "Well," she said, choosing denial as defense. "That's an arrogant attitude, even for you."

"Arrogance has nothin' to do with it. We slept together after Josie's wedding reception. Remember? You, me, acres of moonlight? Bein' pregnant doesn't wipe out your memory, does it? Or is it just selective moments you're forgetting?"

"I remember just fine, thanks. And what I remember is that the night I got pregnant, you weren't even in Wyoming. This baby is mine, Alex. Not yours, so you can quit shaking in your boots. I have no claim on you and neither does my child."

Koby tossed his head, stamped a foot, pulled on the lead, and Alex stopped frowning at her long enough to turn the horse and walk him back toward the corral. Annie stood her ground, watching the worn and faded denim that cupped his butt and emphasized the long, muscular length of his legs, thinking about all the experiences she'd had watching him from this point of view. Walking away from her. Always walking away...even if now he was just walking to the corral to turn the horse loose inside it so he could come back and focus all his attention on arguing with her.

He closed the gate, stood there with one booted foot resting on the bottom rail, watching the horse run off some tension, and just when Annie thought he wasn't coming back to her, he turned and approached her in a long, purposeful stride. "Let's get this straight, Annie. Are you tryin' to tell me I'm not the father of your baby?"

She kept her gaze steady on him, figuring that a lie said straight-out had at least a chance of being believed. "That's just what I'm saying, Alex. This is not your baby."

His jaw tightened, flexed, and she thought he'd probably benefit by a run in the corral, too. But she didn't, of course, say so.

"Then, whose baby is it?" he asked. "And don't say it's yours, 'cause that's not what I'm asking."

"I know what you're asking, Alex, and I'm going to tell you. So listen up and listen up good. The father of this baby is—" she sucked in a deep breath and felt the baby kick in protest "—none of your business."

"You mean to stand there and tell me that I'm not the father, but you're not telling who is?"

"I'm not telling *you*," she stated firmly.

"So Josie knows? Your Uncle Dexter—does he know? What about Genevieve? Hilda Lawson? Doc Wilson? I'll bet he asked and I'll bet you told him, too, didn't ya? That doctor-patient privilege thing?"

"I haven't discussed this with anyone. And for your information, Doc Wilson retired two years ago. Bison City has grown some since the last time you paid any attention to things like doctors and our little hospital. We're getting right uptown around here, Alex. There's a new GP, Dave Gardner, who moved over from Cheyenne a while back. I even have a female obstetrician—and get this, she's pregnant, too. Maybe you ought to go down to her office and ask her who fathered *her* baby!"

Annie hadn't meant to get angry, hadn't realized she *was* angry with him, but suddenly all the times he'd disappointed her welled up into this one worst-case scenario. He could disappoint her until the cows came home, but she'd never, in a million, trillion years give him the opportunity to disappoint her child. Breaking her heart was one thing; breaking the heart of her child was another thing altogether.

Alex took off his hat and dusted it across his thigh. Once, and then again. When he fastened his blue eyes on her, she could see that he was angry, too. Good. She could handle anger. It was sweet-talk she had trouble with.

He pursed his lips. "I'm only interested in what's rightfully mine, Annie."

Anger fled and fear replaced it. He didn't get a say in this. She wouldn't allow it. Not today. And definitely not later. He'd forfeited his right to anything of hers the last time he'd said goodbye. Make that the last three times. "Rest assured, Alex, that I have nothing of yours, except a dog. You'll be happy to know that the dog you hit is recuperating and will probably be ready to go home day after tomorrow. Turns out her owner died, and the dog was lost. I told the vet at the Sheridan clinic that you'd be adopting Footloose just as soon as she's well. Congratulations, you've escaped the bonds of fatherhood only to run smack dab into the responsibilities of pet ownership.''

Alex frowned. ''Footloose?''

''The dog.'' Annie had made up the name on the spot, and thought she'd been downright clever with it, too. ''What a coincidence. Footloose the dog and Footloose the guy. Must be fate that brought the two of you together.''

''I can't take care of that dog, no matter what its name is.''

My point, exactly, Annie thought. ''Then I guess you'll have to find somebody else to adopt her,'' she said. ''Considering you're the one who caused the injury, I'd say that makes her your responsibility.''

''I didn't hit her.'' Alex shoved a hand through his tangled hair and slapped his hat back on his head. ''Can't you keep her?''

''No,'' Annie said in no uncertain terms. ''No. This is something you'll have to take care of yourself. She'll be ready to leave the clinic day after tomorrow, and I will expect you to be here to pick her up, Alex.'' She turned to go back inside, more sure than ever that she was doing the right thing. If he couldn't imagine taking care of a forty-pound dog, how could she ever let him assume any responsibility for a child?

Oh, yes, she was certainly within her rights to lie to him about the baby. And, all things considered, she thought she'd handled this first, difficult confrontation with poise and aplomb.

Even if all she'd really wanted to do, all she still really wanted, was to welcome him home with a kiss that would set his boots on fire.

Chapter Two

This was not the way Alex had thought his day would go.

He'd anticipated an argument, sure. But not with Annie. He hadn't even expected to see her so soon. But here he was, watching her walk away from him, and noting the new swing in her walk, attributing it to the pregnancy, and ultimately wondering how she could handle the often heavy work of doctoring animals. What had happened to Dr. Dex, anyway? He was too old to quit, too ornery to retire. But there was Annie, the only veterinarian anywhere in sight.

Alex supposed he could ask Genevieve, but like as not she wouldn't tell him. Most people said that everything Doc Dex knew about being contrary, he'd learned from Genevieve. Besides, at the moment Alex didn't really care why Annie was working the clinic and her uncle wasn't. He cared that she was going to have a baby. He cared, as well, that she didn't seem to want him to have any part

of it. He cared that she seemed bound and determined to lie right to his face.

This is not your baby, she'd said. Flat-out. As if
she didn't have a doubt about it. Well, he didn't
have any doubts about it, either. It *was* his
baby...no matter what Annie said.

Koby nickered, and Alex looked over at him,
feeling a surge of respect for the magnificent animal. He was flashy, with his quick moves and
tough-guy attitude. He was nearly too smart for his
own good, too, but Alex had seen the potential in
the horse's fluid coordination, the way he responded to voice intonations and the touch of a
human hand. Koby was the best damn cutting
horse Alex had ever seen much less trained. He
had better cow sense than a whole passel of bovine
experts. And he had it despite being the descendent
of rather ordinary parents and in spite of being all
but ruined by his first trainer. Kodiak Blue was an
extraordinary horse, and he was going to have
everyone connected to the quarter horse industry
scratching their heads over his bloodlines while
wondering where in hell he'd come from—and
how in hell Alex had been the one to discover him.

Matt and Jeff would hit the roof when they
found out, of course. They'd agreed, back in April,
that the ranch would finance Alex's foray into the
world of breeding and training cutting horses. Matt
had even studied up on the subject and suggested
a handful of horses Alex might check into buying.
Good horses, all of them, with a lineage traceable
to the biggest money winners in AQHA cutting

history. Alex knew his oldest brother was expecting him to come home with one of those horses, not one that boasted no recognizable lineage and had one heck of a bad reputation to boot. But blood didn't always run true, and a reputation wasn't always a reliable measure of a horse. Or a man, for that matter. Alex knew he'd chosen wisely. He knew that with a couple more months of TLC and persuasive training, Koby would do all that was expected of him and more.

Now, if only Annie could be persuaded to be as responsive. Turning back toward the clinic, Alex weighed his options and found them woefully short on satisfaction. He could follow Annie inside, try to get her to talk to him. He could try the same tack with Genevieve, which was almost guaranteed to be frustrating and embarrassing. Or he could go on out to the ranch and take out his aggravation on whichever brother happened to be there. Matt, probably, but Jeff would do just as well.

Alex rubbed the back of his neck, weary from the long day's driving, the tension of hurrying to get the injured dog to the vet's, seeing Annie for the first time since Josie's wedding, and finding out, too late, that once again he'd missed some very important months in her life. It kept coming back to that. Annie was pregnant and Alex had some questions that needed answerin'. Sooner rather than later.

If Annie wasn't talkin' and it was pretty clear she didn't plan on it, then he'd have to ask elsewhere...and the best person to ask seemed to be his little sister. Josie, who always knew more than she told, but usually told something worth hearing, anyway. He'd just mosey back into the clinic and ask Annie if he could stable his horse at her place for the night. Probably made more sense to talk to Matt first before he took Koby out to the S-J. Give his oldest brother a little time to cool off before he actually saw the horse. And that way Alex would be guaranteed a bona fide excuse to come back later and talk to Annie again…after he'd had time to rephrase the questions and frame his own answers. One way or t'other, he was going to get Annie to admit that he'd had a part in making this baby. Then he'd be on firmer ground when he explained how he intended to have a part in *his* baby's future.

And if that wasn't enough to make a cowboy quake in his boots, Alex just didn't care to know what else it'd take.

"ALEX!" Josie jumped up from the computer, pushed past the swinging, spindle-wood gate that divided the *Bison City Bugle* news staffers from the general public and threw herself into his arms. "When did you get into town?"

He hugged her tight, then stepped back and looked down. She was taller than Annie and carried her pregnancy higher and less out front, but pound for pound, he thought the two women were about at equal roundness. "What're you hidin' under that shirt, Jo? A Halloween pumpkin?"

She laughed, grabbed his hand and made him

pat her stomach. "Say hello to your niece or nephew," she said. "Although as much as the baby's kicking today, it feels like there's one of each in there."

There was a puff of movement beneath his hand and Alex pulled back, uncomfortably aware of how little he knew about what went on inside a woman while a new life formed and grew. "Must be protesting your disastrous taste in radio stations. Sheesh, Josie, haven't I taught you better than to listen to rap music?"

She thumped him lightly on the arm. "That's not rap, you idiot. It's a language tape. I'm teaching the baby to speak French."

"Shucks. I was sort of hoping the little dickens would come out speaking English."

Josie rolled her eyes. "If you had your way, Alex, this baby would come out wearing a cowboy hat and he'd behave just like Clint Eastwood in those old spaghetti Westerns."

"Well, not if it's a girl. I wouldn't want any niece of mine going as long as he did without a bath."

She pinched his arm with well-aged affection. "Your niece or nephew is going to learn something about culture from the world outside of Bison City, Wyoming, and that means the language tape keeps playing."

Alex grinned, loving his dark-haired, optimistic little sister. "Well, if you just want him or her speaking another language, I can teach 'em all they need to know in one easy lesson."

"Oh, sure, you could. And just how much French do you speak?"

"French kiss, French fries and French toast. The three best things ever to come out of France," he said decisively, waiting for her laugh...which came with another jab on his arm.

"It's a good thing you're not around much. Not only would this child pick up your skewed sense of humor, but you'd have Justin's son swaggering all over the place, talking like his redneck uncle."

"I plan on teaching him the real important stuff," Alex agreed. "Like how to persuade his sister to go across the street to the Chuck Wagon Café and partake of a piece of Nell Murphy's cherry pie. With a scoop of cherry vanilla ice cream. Maybe a cup of coffee, too. Heck, I might even tell the little guy that once in a while it's okay to ask his sister for advice."

Instantly intrigued, Josie cocked her dark head to one side. "Advice? You're asking me for advice?"

Alex shrugged. "Depends on whether or not you spring for the coffee and cherry pie."

"You are a card-carrying, bona fide tease, Alex McIntyre," she said. "And I'm so happy to see you I'd pick the cherries, pit 'em and make the pie myself."

"Now, there's a scary thought. Let's just enjoy Nell's home-baked goods and save your energy for gossip." He glanced around the newspaper office, waving to Ramona Helt, who was on the phone, probably trying to convince Asa Mills over at the

Shop'n Stop to take out a quarter-page ad in next week's edition. The rest of the newspaper office was a conjugation of inactive verbs, empty chairs, stacked papers, messy desks—all but one deserted—although to be fair, the *Bugle* had never been a beehive. "Not exactly a hoppin' place," Alex said. "Where is everybody?"

"If you mean our crackerjack reporter, Ned, he's out combing the county for news," she answered as if it should be obvious. "Never know when a big story could break around here, you know."

"Boy, do I. Where's Justin?"

"He's out soliciting advertising for our First Baby of Bison City 2000 contest. I did tell you about the contest, didn't I?"

"I believe you mentioned it, yes," he said, although she'd talked about little else during the whole of their last two telephone conversations.

"I'm just so excited about the whole idea. We only thought of having a contest a few weeks ago, but it's really taken off. I mean, who would have thought our little town would have so many babies due right about the same time? And just as the new millennium begins, too. There's something so…cosmic about the whole thing, don't you think?"

"Either that or someone spiked the water hole with Love Potion #9."

Josie grabbed her wallet and signaled to Ramona that she was going across the street to the café. "Well, whatever prompted this baby boom, it's good for Bison City. The contest is already off and running, and people are talking about it all the time. We're putting together a nice cash prize, plus lots of donated stuff, for the winning mother and baby, plus we're going to raise enough cash to update some of the hospital's antiquated equipment. That way all us mommies-to-be won't have to drive clear into Sheridan to have every little test done."

Alex tugged at his hat brim as he held the door for Josie and followed her outside onto the sidewalk. "Yeah," he said. "I'm real anxious to hear about all these new mommies to be." *One, in particular.* "Just how many would that amount to? All told?"

He caught the glint of calculation in Josie's eyes, noted the way her gaze shifted to him and away, knew she was trying to decide whether to bring up Annie's name. "Let's see, there's me, of course. Then, Barbie Ward. Her baby's really due the first week of December, so she's a real long shot to win the prize. But she wanted to enter, so I count her, too. Then there's Dr. Elizabeth Lee. She's my obstetrician and new to town. You haven't met her. Her due date's in January, but Annie—*I* thought Elizabeth ought to be part of the contest—especially since she'll be delivering most of the babies. So she's in it, too. Then there's Rachel Holcomb. She moved out of the city limits, but she's still in the county, so she counts, too. Plus her due date's the same as mine, December 29. Oh, and you remember Katie Watts, don't you? She and Jimmy

Thomas got married a year ago February, and they're expecting about the same time. I forget her due date, but it's close. And then, just when An— *I* start talking about all the people we know who're pregnant and how maybe we should have some kind of contest or something, the Forsythe twins move back to town with their husbands and guess what?''

"Let me guess." Alex wasn't sure whether he should be impressed by this largesse of the stork or searching the scriptures for a sign. "They're both pregnant, too?"

Josie's smile sparkled with excitement. "Bingo. It's just a baby blizzard. At this rate, we're going to have to post warnings at both ends of Highway 34, warning women not to drink the water."

"It'd be kinder to warn the men that the hormonal levels in Bison City are dangerously high and they might want to detour around town." He looked both ways—more because he'd learned to be a right bit careful while living and driving in San Antonio, than because there was much traffic here—before taking Josie's arm and starting across the street. "Anybody else I ought to know about?" he asked nonchalantly, as if it didn't matter one way or the other. "Anybody claiming *I* might be responsible for this baby boom?"

She didn't answer until they stepped onto the sidewalk in front of the Chuck Wagon Café. "Is there some reason you think you might be responsible?"

He wished she'd laughed, taken his comment as

the joke he half wished it was. "No reason. Just seems like every time I stop off at home, somebody accuses me of not being responsible. Thought I'd make sure which way the wind is blowing, before I go spoutin' off any denials."

"As if anybody believes you when you do," she said.

"There's only a handful of people whose opinions matter to me, anyway." He reached for the door handle, but didn't pull it open just yet. "So, Josie, *is* there anything else I should know?"

She frowned, gazed at him with sympathetic concern. "Annie's pregnant, too, Alex. I sort of thought—hoped, maybe—you already knew that."

He pulled the door open and followed her inside the small restaurant. A pungent blend of onion and fried chicken smells curled around them like smoke from a campfire. The Chuck Wagon couldn't boast great cooking, but it delivered food that was hot, flavorful and filling, in short order. And Nell's pies were the best in the West, bar none.

"I know about Annie," he admitted, once he faced Josie across the speckled red Formica of their tabletop. "I've just come from the clinic. Found a dog hurt on the way into town. Took it in to get fixed up, never even suspecting Annie was working there."

"Doc Dex is having some health problems. Arthritis and sheer orneriness finally took a toll on his energy, in my opinion, anyway. Then about the middle of May, Annie suddenly moved home, and next thing anybody knew, he'd called all his patients to tell them she was in charge and to leave him alone unless it was a dire emergency. And—I'm quoting him now—he'll decide what's dire and what's not. Annie's living in the old house next door to the clinic. She's fixing it up and planning to live there with the baby. It's handy for her, being so close to work and all, but there's a lot to do before the old place will be up to housing an infant." Josie toyed with the toothpick holder, a bird that dipped down and brought up a single toothpick. The novelty item was a genuine antique, a holdover from the sixties. Nell Murphy had probably bought it new. "You just walked in and saw her, huh?" Josie asked gently. "That's when you found out...about the baby?"

Alex shrugged, and knew he didn't fool his sister for a second, knew she saw the hurt he couldn't hide. "I guess that's as good a way to find out as any."

Josie's blue eyes, so much like his own, turned soft with compassion. "I wanted to tell you, Alex, but...well, I just didn't know how to say it over the phone. I kept hoping she'd write and tell you herself."

"Annie's never been one to keep in touch. Not with me, anyway." On that morning last April, he'd left before she was awake. He'd left without a word about coming back. He'd left without sharing his plans, his hopes, his dreams. He'd left without making a commitment or a promise. He'd left her, as he'd done many times before, with no explanation or excuse. He'd just gone, before she could open her eyes and make him stay with a look. One look—that's all it would have taken— and he'd have said to hell with the future.

But in his heart of hearts, Alex nurtured a strict sense of responsibility. He knew he had something to prove—to her, to his brothers, to himself. He knew what he had to do, so he did it, taking the coward's way, leaving her there, knowing she wouldn't be surprised when she awakened alone. He wasn't sure Annie had even been much disappointed to find him gone. She didn't expect any better from him because he'd never given her any cause to.

He'd known she wouldn't write. Or call. Or seek him out. He'd told himself it was for the best, too. He wasn't—never had been—good enough for Annie Thatcher. He'd thought that once he got his future set and proved himself a winner, maybe then he could set about making it all up to her. Courting her slow and proper, the way she deserved. But he hadn't thought there'd be a baby. He hadn't expected she'd say it was none of his business, either.

"Is her due date the same as yours?" he asked because he had to know.

Josie hesitated. "It's the thirtieth. Dr. Elizabeth says she expects one of us to win the contest, although she's made it very clear that babies are pretty hard to predict." Josie paused, plunged on. "So did Annie…say anything to you? About the baby, I mean?"

A basket of tortilla chips appeared with the waitress, and Alex ate a chip before he answered. "She said it isn't mine."

Josie's eyes widened, maybe because the interior of the Chuck Wagon was dim and the smell of Nell's infamous too-hot-tamale chili wasn't. "Oh, Alex, you didn't just ask her that, did you? Straight out? Without giving her a chance to get over the shock of seeing you all of a sudden?"

"She couldn't have been half as shocked as me. I walk in the clinic, with this lump of shepherd in my arms and there she is—round as a July watermelon and acting like it's none of my business."

"Well, is it?" Josie asked with quiet intensity. "Is it your business, Alex?"

His appetite for chips or cherry pie vanished like the endless prairie. "Nah," he drawled, trying to sound supremely indifferent. "It's not my business at all."

Josie opened her mouth to say something—and Alex hoped she was about to knock the chip off his shoulder with an affirmation that the baby was his, that Annie had admitted as much to her. But the waitress returned then, and with a tiny sigh Josie ordered a piece of cherry pie with cherry vanilla ice cream for her brother, who knew he didn't have the stomach to eat it.

ANNIE AND THE BABY had a deal. No late-in-the-day, sugar-high, empty-calorie snacking for her part. No crazy nighttime gymnastics for his. Most of the time they kept the bargain, but desperate times called for desperate measures, and tonight

she needed chocolate. Lots of it. Even if it made
the baby—and consequently, her—restless later on.

Rocking back in the rocking chair on her front
porch, she solemnly unwrapped a Hershey's Kiss
and promised herself she'd only eat the one.
Knowing in her heart ten more were as good as
gone. It might not have been so bad if the mammoth horse trailer wasn't right there in plain sight,
backed up next to the holding pen, glinting at her
like a silver tooth, reminding her that Alex Mc-
Intyre was home.

Home. Ha! As if he knew the meaning of the
word. She'd known he would come around, sooner
or later. She'd just hoped it would be after the baby
was born. After she'd established the parental
bonds. After she'd met her son and assured herself
that she could be not only his mother, but his father
as well. That was the other part of their deal, hers
and the baby's. She hadn't done so great at choosing his father, so she'd step up to the plate and fill
that role, too. Much better for a child to have one
responsible parent than…what? Than one irresponsible one? Or one of each? Well, her son wasn't
going to know he had a choice. It was her or nothing. So he was stuck with her.

The early signs of an autumn sunset were just
touching the mountain-scalloped horizon with a
hint of muted color, and overhead the first stars
sparked in faint, eager twinkles, unable to wait for
the indigo backdrop of night to blanket the sky.
''Pretty,'' she told the child in her womb, talking
softly to him as she was wont to do when there

was no one else around. "Once you get here, you'll want to spend a lot of time watching the sunset. Sunrise is pretty, too, but it'd be nice if you saved those until you're older and I'm caught up on my sleep."

The baby made no move in response, keeping his part of the bargain, and with a sigh Annie rocked back and forth, savoring the texture and taste of the chocolate, even though she knew she'd pay for the pleasure later on. But wasn't that the story of her life? Wasn't that exactly how she'd wound up pregnant? One starry, romance-drenched night last April, she'd decided to say a last and final goodbye to Alex by giving herself an unforgettable fantasy before getting on with her life. At the time she'd considered making love with him worth whatever happened later.

Of course, she'd thought that "whatever" would be basically limited to the disappointment of waking up alone, which she'd expected. Not to getting pregnant, which she hadn't. That was the kick fate had delivered square to the seat of her pants. Just when she'd gotten the courage to put Alex out of her life, presto, her reproductive system got ideas all its own. The last laugh, of course, was hers. She hadn't bargained for a baby, a moment-by-moment reminder that a part of Alex would be in her life forever, but it wasn't a bad trade. Not a bad trade, at all.

The geriatric sputter of a worn-out motor warned her that he was returning, even before she saw the battered old truck turn into the drive that ran between the clinic and the house. She'd known he'd be back tonight to check on his horse, knew part— if not all—of the reason he'd wanted to stable the animal overnight was so he'd have an excuse to confront her again. Well, she was ready for him. Fortified by the knowledge she had almost a full bag of chocolate kisses, she figured he was as good as vanquished before he ever got around to opening his big mouth.

He got out of the truck, stood there staring at the Bighorn Mountains, absorbing the first orange-red rays of the coming sunset, then swept off his hat in a flawlessly unconscious gesture, as if he couldn't help but acknowledge that such heart-pinching beauty demanded a show of respect. Which was always the problem with Alex McIntyre. Just when she convinced herself he had not a smidgen of appreciation for a sunset, he went and took off his hat, making her wonder if maybe— just maybe—she was wrong. About sunsets. And sons. And what it took to be a daddy worth having.

"Evenin'," he said, glancing over at her on the porch. "Just came back to get Koby settled for the night."

"Really?" She renewed her rocking, more to keep from fidgeting than anything else. "I figured you came back just to aggravate me."

His grin topped the list of her favorite smiles. "And here I took it for granted I was doing that just by breathing the sweet air of Wyoming."

"Well, there's your trouble...thinking I care if you're breathing."

He laughed, and if a sound could hold color and texture, Alex's laughter would have been the white of moonlight and had the feel of a roughly woven tapestry. "Ah, Annie, 'fess up. You're happy to see me."

"I'm happy to see your horse eating his head off in my barn. With what you owe me for your dog, I'm gonna be real happy to cash your check."

Alex shut the door of the truck and walked toward her. There was always purpose in his stride and yet at the same time an innuendo that he had nowhere else to go and nothing else to do. In his blue eyes was the suggestion she was the only woman in the world with whom he could imagine sharing a sunset...and a sunrise. Providing, of course, something better didn't come along between one and the other. Annie knew better than to believe this time was any different from a dozen times before. But every time he came near her—every single time—her silly heart behaved like a blushing adolescent, stammering, halting, rushing to greet him with wild and raw delight. She drew a deep breath. Sherlock Holmes had had his Moriarty. Napoleon, his Waterloo. Annie had Alex.

Except this time, she had someone else to think about. Alex's son. A tiny little heart beating fast with the hope that she could, and would, protect him.

"We need to talk." Alex came up the steps to the porch and perched on the rail, leaning a muscular shoulder against the support post, crossing his arms as if he dared her to tell him to get lost.

Annie wanted to, she really did, but that would accomplish only one thing—the assurance that he'd stick to that railing like glue. She had experience handling Alex. That much, at least, was in her favor. "What about?"

"You, me…the baby."

Sighing, she crossed her arms, too, then immediately uncrossed them, not wanting to draw his attention to her rounded stomach. "There is no 'you and me,'" she said firmly. "And that means we positively are not going to talk about my baby. *My* baby, Alex. Mine."

"Oh, come on, Annie. I may not be an obstetrician, but I can count the months from April to October as well as you can. We slept together at the first of April, and in October you're six months pregnant. Why not just admit the baby's mine and let's get on with deciding what we're going to do about it?"

She thought about hitting him with the flat of her hands and knocking him off the porch. But that would require a quick get-up-and-go from the rocking chair and, unfortunately these days, she was in a more push-up-and-pull stage of mobility. "It's just like you, Alex, to show up unexpectedly and try to wheedle your way back into my good graces. What surprises me this time is how you seem to be so eager to take on a responsibility that rightfully belongs to someone else."

He took a second to set his hat on his thigh and settle it carefully there before his gaze came up to pin her with the question. "And just who is responsible, Annie? Besides you, that is."

"Just me."

"Not satisfactory. It takes two to create a baby, and if you're determined to convince me I had nothing to do with creating this one, then you're going to have to give me a name, a face and a dadgum social security number."

"I don't think so." She'd stopped rocking, started clenching the arms of the rocking chair, begun to worry that he would never believe her. "I don't think I have to give you the time of day."

"Then, how about you tell me whether it was the week before Josie's wedding or the week after that you fell into bed with another man. I figure the window of opportunity for making a baby is still fairly narrow."

"That's insulting."

"Damn straight it is. Give it up, Annie. You don't sleep around, and I know for a fact you don't fall for any old line."

"Oh, so since I fell for yours, that automatically cancels out falling for someone else?"

"Yes." He looked confident, sure of himself, altogether too handsome for his own good. Or hers. "You wouldn't have come from another man's arms to mine, Annie. And you wouldn't have gone straight from mine to somebody else's. We made a baby...and I'm trying to do the right thing by it."

"He," she corrected. "It's a boy. I had an ultrasound last week and the sex of the baby was pretty clear.''

He looked stunned, as if she'd hit him with all four aces. "A son." He swallowed hard and visibly. "We'll need to get married."

She had to put an end to this fantasy. It wasn't going to work. Not in a million years. No matter how good his intentions at this moment, it wasn't going to work. "I'll say this again, Alex. My son. Mine, not yours. And marriage isn't a mistake I care to make at this time in my life." Pushing to her feet—no easy task—she stood and he slid from the rail to stand too, towering over her like a cross between the Grim Reaper and John Wayne. "I don't know what it's going to take to make you believe me. I don't really care if you do or not. I just want you to go away again and leave me alone. That's clear enough, isn't it?''

"You don't mean that."

"Oh, yes, I do."

"There's only one thing you can say that will make me leave. If I'm not the father of your baby, then tell me who is. A name. The circumstances. How it happened you were so in love with him, you made love with me at almost the same moment in time?''

Annie could feel the trembling start, the aching to cast caution aside and make her bed with Alex. Forever and ever, amen. But it wouldn't be just her bed. It would be her son's, too. And the trouble was, Alex wouldn't be in it most of the time. He'd be off to parts unknown, chasing yesterday's promise, telling himself he'd be there for her tomorrow. And if he wasn't off somewhere, he'd resent her and her son for the tender trap in which they'd caught, and kept, his heart. She had planted a painful goodbye last spring. It was her responsibility now to make sure it took root. "Not everything can be had for the asking, Alex. I've told you the truth. This is not your child. You can sit on this porch until the cows come home, but it won't change anything. You've practiced plenty at taking the easy way out, so why balk now? Go back wherever you've been and forget what happened between us six months ago."

A rueful slant of a smile appeared at the corner of his lips. "Now, why would I want to forget one minute of the time I've spent with you, Annie? And even if I wanted to, what makes you think I could?"

"Experience, Alex," she said as she opened the screen door. "Lots of experience."

Then, keeping a tight rein on her resolve, she went in and closed the door behind her, shutting him outside with the last of the sunset—and, darn it, all of her chocolate kisses.

Chapter Three

He couldn't tell for sure, but Alex thought the door hit her in the butt, she was in such a hurry to shut him out. So here he was, alone on her porch, talking to her in his head as if she was still there arguing with him. Frustrating woman. All he wanted to do was help her. She needed help, damn it. Any fool could see that. This house needed more fix-up than a few cans of paint could provide. From what Josie had said and what he'd observed earlier in the day, Annie was handling the clinic without much assistance from her uncle. Either job would offer up any number of problems even before factoring in her pregnancy and her apparent determination to make it to motherhood all on her own.

Stubborn, she was. Webster's dictionary probably listed Annie as a prime example of obstinate, too. He'd come right out and told her he'd marry her, do the right thing, and still she'd declared the baby wasn't his, wouldn't be his even if he waited until the cows came home. Annie had cows, too. At least, her Uncle Dex did. He grazed quite a few head on the acres back of the clinic. Had for years. So it wasn't as if she didn't know the cows came home for feeding every evening like clockwork, as if in some roundabout way she was inviting him to stay.

Alex knew he was grasping at straws, but he hadn't expected her to keep denying the obvious. The baby was his. No matter what she said.

Unless…it wasn't.

But how could that be? Annie wouldn't have— On the other hand, she might have. Hadn't he told her often enough that she ought to? Hadn't he teased her about getting herself a real boyfriend back when he was too stupid to realize she actually might? Wouldn't it serve him right if she'd finally taken his advice?

Okay, so he didn't deserve Annie. What else was new? That wasn't the question, anyway. If there was another man, where was he? Why wasn't he here with her? What kind of fool would leave Annie once he knew she loved him? Releasing his breath in a self-deprecating rush, Alex knew exactly what kind of fool that man would be.

On the other hand, she'd only shut the door. She hadn't said she was never speaking to him again. And if he sat on her porch and ate the chocolate she'd left out—well, sooner or later, she'd come out and fuss at him. How did he know that?

Experience. Lots of experience.

ANNIE PULLED ASIDE one small section of the sheet that hung over the parlor window and peeked out.

He was still there, sitting in her rocking chair, his boots propped on the porch railing, eating Hershey's Kisses one by one and dropping the silver wrappers in his lap. At the rate he was popping them, she wouldn't have to worry about those empty calories. No, sir.

Didn't he know better than to irritate an expectant mother? Didn't he know pregnant women were often dangerously hormonal? Didn't he have somewhere he needed to be? Someplace other than her front porch? Why couldn't he just go take care of his horse and leave? It wasn't as if he didn't have the whole S-J ranch house porch to sit on. It wasn't as if he couldn't stop on his way to the ranch and buy his own Hershey's Kisses. It wasn't as if he had to chow down on her one and only bag.

Before she quite knew her own intentions, Annie jerked open the door, retaining just enough practicality to stay safely behind the screen. "Give me that candy," she said.

He acknowledged her presence by unwrapping another piece, tossing the chocolate into his mouth, and dropping the foil onto his lap. " Eat an orange," he said congenially. "You need the vitamin C."

"Eat dirt and die," she countered, which wasn't exactly what she'd meant to say, but seemed expressive enough in a pinch.

"You talk turkey and I'll consider it." He leisurely unwrapped another candy and smiled at her while he did it. Even diffused by a good-size patch of wire-mesh screen, the slant of that smile made her knees go all soft and tingly. Why couldn't she have found Clarence Tompkins charming all those years ago in eighth grade? He'd had a huge crush on her back then. Why couldn't he have been the one to tell Jason Kittredge to stick a sock in his mouth? Why did it have to be Alex who took her side? Alex, the one her heart chose to be a hero?

"I'm not talking to you," she said firmly, although he had to know as well as she did that was nothing more than bravado. "Now, give me what's left of that candy and go torment somebody else."

"This candy?" He held up the bag. "Trust me, you don't want this. It's got way too many empty calories for a woman in your condition."

"My condition needs calories. Lots of them. Chocolate is just what the doctor ordered."

"I'll bet he doesn't know you're substituting chocolate for a real meal, does he?"

Guilty. Not that she planned to admit today's poor eating habits to him or Dr. Elizabeth. "She." Annie redirected in self-defense. "I believe I already told you that my obstetrician is a woman."

"You mentioned it, yes. Accused me of being the father of her baby, as I recall."

"I did not. You seemed to want to take the responsibility for somebody's baby and I merely suggested you talk to her."

"I'm thinkin' I'll make an appointment." He rolled the spent wrappers into a small silver ball and dropped it into the cellophane bag with the untouched candy. Then he folded the whole bag—

what was left of it—into a tight little package and
set it on the floor, where she'd have to either walk
all the way around the porch or get down on her
knees and crawl under his propped-up, lazy pair of
legs to get her hands on it. "Ask her about pater-
nity tests and stuff like that," he continued, oblivious to her dilemma. "Never too early to plan
ahead."

Annie felt hungry all of a sudden...and edgy
about what Alex might do. Not a happy combination. "For the last time, you are not about to
become a daddy. Not with this baby, anyway. So
why don't you quit hassling me about it?"

"I'm figuring the father must be somebody I
know, since you're so determined not to name
names."

She wondered why she hadn't simply told him
the truth in the first place, then remembered the
consequences. "That is a giant leap of logic," she
said. "Even for you."

"Maybe, but I think I could be on the right track
here. Let me just take a stab at guessing." He
dropped his feet from the railing to the floor and
scooted forward in the chair so he could make eye
contact. "Harvey Mellencamp."

"Harvey—? Are you nuts? That old coot is old
enough to be my grandfather."

"Maybe even your great-grandfather, but I'm
working my way down the list of Bison City bachelors, and I had to start somewhere." Alex
stopped, frowned, rubbed his chin. "I am right in
sticking with bachelors, I take it?"

"You can read names out of the phone book if you want, but I am not having this discussion with you."

"You can end it anytime, Annie. Just tell me what I want to know."

She was tempted to march out there and tell him everything. How panicked she'd been at the first hint she might be pregnant. How ridiculously happy she'd been in the first astonishing moments after finding out she was. How quickly the worry set in. How hard the questions got. How much everything changed. It would have been nice to have had someone—him—to talk to. It would have been reassuring to know he was there for her to depend on for support, help and plain old encouragement. It wouldn't have made the decisions easier, necessarily, but it would have been nice to share them and not shoulder all the burden alone.

But Alex hadn't been there. "I'm going to go into the kitchen and fix myself something green and disgustingly healthy, and if that bag of candy is gone when I come back out to get it, you're going to owe me twice the normal boarding rate for your animals. Are we clear on that?"

He pursed his lips, rubbed a fingertip across his jaw. "Stanley Hillman?"

She rolled her eyes.

"Tyson Thomas, then."

As if she would let that one pass. "Don't be completely ridiculous. His mother would never let him date a redhead, much less a woman who can't cook."

"Poor old Tyson will never know what he missed." Alex smiled, softly and slow. "Because I seem to recall you cook up a mean picnic supper."

She blushed, damn it. And not from embarrassment, either, but pleasure—pure, sweet pleasure—that he remembered. Not that he had any business knowing her memories of him were anything but aggravating. "I should have poisoned those barbecue ribs when I had the chance."

"Life is full of missed opportunities," he said with a shrug. "Okay, what about Jack Pannell? He was forever after you to two-step with him at the VFW Howdy dances."

"Jack moved to Cheyenne several years ago, when his daughter, Eleanor—who, in case you've forgotten, went to school with my Uncle Dex—decided he couldn't take care of himself anymore and put him in a rest home."

"I know you're too sassy for old Jack to handle. I meant his son, Eleanor's youngest brother. Isn't his name Jack, too?"

"John," she corrected. "And he's been married for years."

"Is that a fact?" Alex stood, tall, lean, about the most compelling reason for Wrangler jeans she'd ever seen on her front porch. "Hmm. Looks like I'm going to have to brush up on who is and isn't still a bachelor around here."

"Times change," she said. "People change. Nothing stays the same. You should know that by now."

He scratched his head, pushing his hat to a rakish tilt in the process. "If you're turning philosophical, I must be getting warm."

"I don't understand why it matters to you who the father of this baby is, Alex. It's not like I'm asking you to be responsible."

"I'm sorta thinkin' I am, though, see, and unless I find out differently, I mean to *be* responsible. Are we clear on that?" His gaze tussled some with hers, and she went down in defeat, losing the battle if not the war.

"He's not from Bison City," she said, hoping her expression was sad enough, weary enough, wary enough to be convincing. "Not that that's any of your business, either."

"Well now, that's just what we're trying to determine, isn't it?" He glanced down at the scuffed toes of his Tony Llama boots, as if he was feeling a bit guilty for pressuring her, but no such luck. "Where is he? In the house, there, with you?"

"You know he's not."

"Are you expecting him anytime soon?"

"No." She searched for inspiration, tried to think of some little detail that might convince him. "He's…in the Peace Corps."

"The Peace Corps?"

Annie had to defend the father of her child, even if she had made him up on the spot. "What's wrong with that? He's a very unselfish person."

"He must be quite a guy. How'd you meet him?"

"Um...in school. He was at Kansas State with me."

"He's a veterinarian, too?"

She nodded, eager to collaborate any idea he might have about her imaginary mate. "Yes."

"Did he know he was going to become a father before he so unselfishly joined the Peace Corps?"

"No." She hesitated, realizing this was going to get complicated. "I...uh, didn't find out until he'd left. For Africa. He's in Africa."

Alex nodded, as if that made perfect sense. "Stands to reason the Peace Corps would need veterinarians in Africa."

"That's not what he does," she snapped, and immediately regretted it because she had only the vaguest idea of what the Peace Corps did do in Africa or anywhere else. "He's...building houses."

"That's noble, considering you're here trying to turn a rundown old house into a home for his baby. When's he coming back?"

"He's not."

Alex frowned. "Ever?"

Oops. "Not for a while," she corrected, smiling, thinking she must be crazy to have started this. "Quite a while." Alex looked even more doubtful, so she added, "But he'll be here before the baby's born. He promised."

"A man would want to be there when his son's born."

"Yes." She swallowed hard. "He wouldn't want to miss that."

"I wouldn't, if it was me."

"No, of course you wouldn't. If it was you. Which it's not. See? I told you you're trying to borrow someone else's trouble. Now you can go on about your business knowing this is not your problem."

He rubbed his chin and a good twenty-four hours worth of stubby beard. If she hadn't known the story of Samuel and Jocasta McIntyre, hadn't heard the tale of how Samuel had let a fortune in gold sink to the ocean floor off Cape Horn in order to save the woman he loved and later married, if it wasn't common knowledge that Sam and Jocasta had eventually settled in Wyoming and started a dynasty, well, it would have been easy to believe that Alex was descended from the most notorious outlaws ever to inhabit the nooks and crannies of the Bighorn Mountains. He looked the part. Outlaw to the core. Audacious. Handsome. I'll-take-that attitude. And as likely to steal her heart as hold it hostage.

"Here's what I'm thinking, Annie," he said after a short silence. "That's not much of a story."

He didn't believe a word she'd said. Lied. Okay she'd lied and he knew it. So what? Lifting her chin, she brazenly asked, "What part bothers you?"

"Pretty much everything except you being pregnant and not telling the man who got you that way."

"Look, I'm not going to stand here and argue. I've worked all day. I have a date with a can of paint tonight and, since you ate all the chocolate, I'm now faced with fixing myself something completely unappetizing to eat.''

"You're hungry?"

She nodded. "Yeah, I am.''

"So am I. I'll fix you something. Something hot and nourishing and a thousand times better for you than Hershey's Kisses.''

"But not as good.''

"Who said? Turn me loose in the kitchen and you'll be begging for my recipes.'' He pulled on the handle of the screen door, but she held fast to the latch. "Plus,'' he said, adding what he obviously felt would be the pièce de résistance, "I'm real handy with a paintbrush.''

Okay, so she was a direct descendent of the pantywaist bank teller who took one look at the dangerous outlaw and turned over all the money in the cash drawer, then offered to open the safe just to be polite. It was sad, really. Embarrassing even. But as she stepped aside, allowing him to open the screen door and walk right back into her life, all she felt was a familiar, deep-down joy that he was here. She'd been lonely for a long time, and when Alex set out to charm her, there was simply nobody who was better equipped for the job. "I won't eat green beans,'' she warned. "No matter how you disguise them.''

He grinned like the thief of hearts he was. "Sounds like a challenge to me. Point me toward the kitchen, Annie, and then stay out of my way.''

As if she hadn't been trying.

SHE NEVER EVEN KNEW he put the green beans in the salad. Chopped up fine and sprinkled in with the parsley. She ate it all and asked for seconds and Alex, through some divine intervention, managed to keep his mouth shut. About green beans and parenthood, if not much else.

He laid his fork across his plate and watched her put away the last of a generous helping of meat loaf and mashed potatoes, marveling that her appetite had outpaced his from the first bite. It must be true that she was eating for two. On the other hand, Annie had always had the metabolism of an adolescent boy. Even the few extra pounds of pregnancy had merely rounded the angles of her body into a pleasing fullness. Once, during their high school Senior Spring Fling, he'd conned her into entering the pancake competition, where she'd handily outeaten Rick, The Moose, Rodman and won the respect of every boy in school. The girls mostly thought she cheated, but they were just jealous. Or hungry.

"Quit staring." She folded her napkin over the remaining bits of the meal, giving it a decent burial. "Haven't you ever seen a pregnant woman eat before?"

"I watched Josie put away a monster slice of cherry pie this afternoon, along with close to a pint of cherry vanilla ice cream."

Annie's eyes brightened hopefully. "Did you make dessert?"

"Tonight?" He laughed. "No, with the state of starvation your cabinets are in, I think I worked a miracle just coming up with a halfway-balanced meal which, I might add, you seemed to enjoy."

"Can't always believe what you see."

"You practically licked the plate."

"I was hungry. You ate all my candy." She brushed a couple of crumbs from her shirt. "I'm surprised you had any appetite left."

"I didn't eat all of it." He gathered up the plates and carried them to the sink. "If you can find the bag, you can have what's left."

"Oh, gee, thanks, Alex. What a guy. Sheesh. You had no right to hide the candy, you know. That was a low-down, dirty rotten trick."

"Yes, it was. I'm thoroughly ashamed of myself."

"Right. As if you even know the meaning of regret."

"Sure I do. It means 'to gret again.' See? I told you those five years at Florida State was time well spent."

"I never doubted it for a minute, despite the fact that you didn't get around to completing a degree."

The words pinched, even though he knew Annie hadn't meant them as criticism. He was overly sensitive, inured to the idea that he was less of a McIntyre than his older brothers, that he lacked the sense of responsibility both Matt and Jeff held as an unconscious, but sacred trust. He, on the other hand, had rebelled early and often, trying always to separate his identity from his actions.

Not finishing the few hours needed for that piece

of sheepskin, however, was probably the dumbest bit of defiance he'd ever pulled. It didn't really matter that he'd eventually taken the couple of classes necessary for the degree and obtained the official document. He'd cheated himself out of any celebratory graduation, sacrificed the moment when he might have basked in genuine family pride, and consequently, he hadn't mentioned his accomplishment to anyone. It hadn't seemed important...until now. "I finished the degree," he said as he stooped to look inside the cabinet under the sink. "Where's the sink stopper?"

"What?"

"You know, the round, rubber mat that keeps the water from going down the drain?"

"I know what a sink stopper is." Her chair scraped on the old vinyl flooring as she got up from the table. "What did you say about finishing the degree?"

He wished he hadn't mentioned it. "I finished," he said with a shrug. "No big deal."

"You went back to school?"

"Couple of years ago, I was training Western pleasure horses for a breeder in Florida and I had a little time on my hands. The college was an easy commute, so I took the classes. Here it is." He straightened, holding the sink stopper up for her to see. "I found it."

"I'm proud of you, Alex."

The unfeigned pleasure in her voice pinched his heart...but in a way altogether better than before.

"It wasn't hard," he said. "It had just fallen behind the can of scouring powder."

A light smile curved her lips. "Still, without that diploma, who knows how long it might have taken you to get the dishes done."

"Well, with or without a college degree, it'll take twice as long if you don't grab a dish towel and help."

"I didn't ask you to make a mess in here, you know. I would have been perfectly content with frozen pizza."

He grimaced, hoping she was joking. "A hot meal is much better for you, Annie."

"Well, I don't normally eat the pizza straight out of the freezer." Pulling open a drawer, she rummaged until she withdrew a threadbare, red-checked dish towel. "And I never have to worry about finding little chunks of green beans in it, either. That's a definite plus on the side of pizzas."

"Okay, so I put some green beans in the salad," he admitted. "You ate them."

"No, I picked them out when you weren't looking and dropped them on the floor." With a saucy flip of the towel, she indicated a little pile of chopped green under the table. "You'll want to sweep the floor once you're done with the dishes."

"Annie, Annie, Annie. I had no idea you needed so much looking after."

"That's because I don't. I'm perfectly capable of taking care of myself—and have done so for years. Don't go thinking I need any help from you, because tonight was a one-shot deal. You just caught me in a weak moment and if you hadn't bragged about knowing your way around a paint-brush, you wouldn't be here now.''

He smiled, loving her spirit, but completely un-fazed by her declaration of independence. In fact, he was as tickled as a little boy pulling a dog's tail to discover just how much she needed his help. Reaching across, he turned on the hot water, squirted some liquid soap into the sink and watched the bubbles rise. First thing, he decided, she needed an automatic dishwasher. It'd be real easy to install one, and then she'd be able to ster-ilize the baby bottles without boiling them. A dish-washer would cost her a cabinet under the counter, but she had space for a pantry out in the screened-in back porch. He'd have to close in the porch, of course, but that wouldn't be difficult. Just take a little time. There might even be room to put a washer and dryer out there, too. The whole thing would have to be heated, of course, but— Sud-denly the faucet sprang a leak and sprayed him with hot water.

''Oh, I forgot to warn you, Alex. You have to turn the faucet like this...'' She reached past him and jiggled both water taps. ''Or else you'll be dripping wet before the sink is half-full.''

He rubbed the spot on his shirt with a dish towel. ''You need to get that fixed.''

''You think? Gee, wonder why that idea never occurred to me.''

He acknowledged her sarcasm with a wry frown.

"How long have you been living out here, anyway?"

"Off and on over the summer, but full-time since September. Had to wait to move in until Ray Shields got the plumbing to work. He's one very busy plumber these days. Or so he tells me. He's supposed to have ordered a part for the faucet that'll fix the leak, but so far it hasn't come in."

"I'll talk to him, get him to put a rush on it."

"Thanks, but I've got things under control, and if anyone is going to rush the plumber, I'll do it."

"You're paying him, Annie. Just call him up and tell him if he doesn't have it done by tomorrow, you'll get somebody else to do it."

She put her hands on her hips. "I'm not paying him, Alex. We're bartering. He fixes the pipes. I fix his animals. That way I can afford to have plumbing that actually works."

"I take it Uncle Dex isn't offering you much in the way of cash."

"Uncle Dex has been very generous. He's selling me his practice at a very reasonable price and, except for the pastureland, which he's keeping, he threw in this house and the rest of the buildings for much less than he could have gotten from somebody else. If he hadn't, I'd probably still be living in my office."

"He should have given you the whole place, lock, stock and barrel."

The lines around her mouth told him she wouldn't discuss her uncle. "He gave me more than I can ever repay when he took me in after my parents died. I know he's gruff and on the critical side, but he's all the family I have, and he's never been anything but kind to me from the start.''

Dex Thatcher wasn't an easy man to describe, but *kind* wouldn't have made anybody's short list of adjectives. He'd agreed to take his orphaned eight-year-old niece as soon as he heard it was his place or foster care. But providing food, clothing and a roof over her head seemed to have been the extent of his commitment. It was a wonder Annie had turned out as well as she did. ''I wish I could—''

''You can't, Alex. I'm lucky to have what I have, and believe me, I know it.'' Her eyes fixed on him, her words came clear, concise and steady. ''I'm happy with my life just the way it is.'' She paused, then repeated, ''Exactly the way it is.''

It was pointless to tell her she needed him. He'd have to prove it to her a little at a time. Like with the green beans. She may have picked out most of them, but he'd wager she'd eaten enough to do her some good. He was good for Annie, too. No matter how much she protested, no matter how many imaginary Peace Corps heroes she made up. She needed him and he was staying in her life…and in his son's. ''Does that mean you want me to leave the dishes the way they are?'' he asked. ''Because it won't break my heart to jump right into the painting.''

She almost managed to disguise a sigh, but he knew her too well, knew that somehow in that moment of suggesting an unsavory truth, he'd lost a good piece of the ground it'd taken him all evening to gain. "Go take care of your horse, McIntyre. I'll do the dishes and save the painting for another day."

"Koby is already set for the night. I did that while the meat loaf was cooking." He rolled up his shirtsleeves and began washing a plate, sorry he'd given her an opening for any other option. "I'll have your kitchen spick-and-span quicker than two shakes of a heifer's tail."

"Alex?" She reached over and took hold of the dishrag in his hand. "I'd really rather do it myself, thanks. Besides, you know they're waiting for you out at the ranch, wondering what's keeping you."

"If the Bison City grapevine is as solid as its reputation, they know where I am, who I'm with and how much I weigh—with and without my boots on." He held on to the dishrag, but she held on, too, and dishwater dripped into the sink and ran down his arm in soapy rivulets. "I'm not leaving the dishes for you, Annie, so forget it. It'll only take a few minutes to do them."

"I'm pregnant," she said. "Not sick. I can wash dishes. I do it every day."

"So this is one day you don't have to. Read a magazine or something. Take a bath. Wash your hair. Go back to doing whatever you did while I was cooking. I don't care, just please let me wash the dishes tonight." He didn't know why it seemed so important, but staying in her kitchen a little while longer seemed tantamount to staying in her life from now on. Plus, he didn't really want to go home. Matt would only want to talk about cutting horses, breeding and training them, and Alex wanted only to talk about Annie. No, scratch that. He wanted to talk to her. All night. All day tomorrow. Until she admitted under oath that her baby was his, and his baby hers. He wanted to touch her stomach and feel the puff of movement that meant his son was there and growing. He wanted to kiss her, too. To taste the remembered sweetness of her lips and let her know he still found her desirable. More now than ever. He wanted to hold her in his arms while she slept and he wanted to fix her coffee—no, caffeine in any form was probably not a good idea—milk, then. He'd fix her a glass of hot milk—even though that sounded plenty disgusting now, much less first thing in the morning. But whatever she wanted, he'd fix for her. Breakfast? No problem. Well, it wouldn't be, once he replenished her cupboards and refrigerator, filled in the gap between empty and what few canned goods the last renter must have left behind. Whatever it took, he just wanted to be here with her and make up for all the times he hadn't been. "Let me finish what I started here" is what he said.

She let go of the dishrag, and her end dropped like a rock into the water, splashing soap suds across the front of his shirt. "If you insist." Wiping her hands on the dish towel, she tossed it onto the counter next to the sink. "I'll go over to the clinic and check on Loosey."

"Sick goose?" he asked, tearing his thoughts

away from her lips…the soft, kissable curve of her lips.

"Loosey is your dog, Alex. Remember?"

"I thought his name was Footless."

"Her name is Footloose. Loosey, for short," she corrected, patting his arm as if he were a forgetful old fool who couldn't remember the name of a dog…or the way a woman's naked body felt wrapped around his.

He brought his hand out of the water and laid it, wet and warning, over hers. "You're not flirting with me, are you, Annie?"

Awareness flashed in the depths of her green eyes, and beneath his palm her skin felt heated and taut. But she didn't let on like she noticed, didn't even pull her hand away from his. Instead, she gave her thick red hair a toss and smiled up at him, serenely and sensuously, obviously brave in the face of his considerable cowboy charm. "Now, why would I do something that stupid, Alex, when I've already told you I'm in love with someone else."

He smiled back, unfazed by her boast. "Oh, right. The hero. Does this Peace Corps paragon have a name?"

"Yes," she said, "he does." Then easily withdrawing from his touch, she waltzed over to the cabinet where the canned goods were kept, reshuffled the vegetables, and pulled the bag of Hershey's Kisses from behind a very large, very dusty can of green beans. Tossing her prize in the air, she caught it with one hand and headed for the door. "I'd offer to share my dessert," she said. "But there's only enough left for me. You can have an orange, though, if you can find one."

Then she sashayed out the door, leaving him alone with his thoughts and the dirty dishes.

Chapter Four

"You get in this house right this minute!" Willie was motioning to Alex from beneath the soft yellow light of the back porch even before he braked the pickup to a complete stop. It was funny, he thought, how over the years her hair had gone gray, she'd picked up a few wrinkles and a few more pounds, but what she yelled was word for word the same, with merely a change in the prime directive. *You get in this house right this minute...and eat your dinner! You get in this house right this minute...and clean your room! You get in this house right this minute...and do your chores...finish your homework...put some hot chocolate in your belly!* Rain or shine. Trouble or good graces. Willie's *You get in this house right this minute...* had called him home a million times.

Home.

Newly capped in faraway white, the Bighorns faded into the gray-blue distance, a view Alex privately believed Mother Nature had sculpted exclusively for him. In every other direction plains rolled into the crescendo of darkness, a muted carpet of autumn color blending into a winter night. Livestock in coats growing shaggy and coarse were dark shapes in the pasture, some still and sleeping, some in search of leftover summer grasses. A crisp breeze heckled the trees and plants in passing, bending close to whisper, "Cold weather coming. Sleep, sleep."

It mattered not that night had fallen, Alex knew this country like the inside of his skin. He knew it by dawn and dark and every hour in between. He knew it through each season, through sun and rain, storm and snow. Each time he returned, each time he was here in this spot, halfway between the wild, wild west and modern civilization, sitting in whatever vehicle he happened to have parked between the S-J barns and the ranch house, back from wherever it was he'd been, Alex knew with the force of an arrow through the center of his soul that he was home.

"What are you yelling about, Wilhemina?" He grinned at her as he grabbed his duffel and slammed the pickup door. "Can't you see I'm home?"

"You get in this house right this minute and hug my neck!" She shifted from foot to foot, bobbing with excitement as he strode up the steps two at a time to reach the porch. Then he was being hugged within an inch of his life, surrounded by her welcome and the tea rose fragrance she'd worn since birth. Well, his birth, anyway.

"It's about time you got here," she said, smiling

with toothy happiness, wiping a trace of a tear from under her blue eyes. "Josie called about six-thirty wantin' to talk to you, and that's the first I knew you were coming home." She gripped his arm with both hands and steered him inside the house. "Where've you been, young'un? I put a plate up for you, saved back a hunk of my Sin-Full chocolate cake. You're hungry, I expect, after that long trip."

He could hardly break her heart by telling her he hadn't driven straight through from Texas without a stop. "Are you kidding? I could probably put away that whole cake and still have room for the crumbs." He hugged her ample waist, untying her apron sash in the process, but when he tried to fix it, she batted him away and simply took the apron off.

"You're not company," she said. "But I guess as how I can take off my apron and sit a spell all the same. Now you sit down and I'll get you that cake."

Alex sat, taking his usual place at the long, pinewood table, inhaling the scents, absorbing the familiar sights, relaxing into the memories of growing from child to man in this kitchen. The whole S-J Ranch house had been modernized over the years, added on to and made more convenient as the McIntyre legacy grew. But the kitchen was still oversize, the heart of the home, the place for family meetings and meals, the one room where ranch hands and family blended into one entity, the ranch.

He loved the smells of hearty food that had assimilated into the walls for nearly eighty years, the weathered cedar beams stained dark from the heat of cooking so many meals. As a child, he'd spent a lot of time in the corner of this room, doing penance for one boyish misdeed or another. He was convinced that's why he liked to cook: he'd experienced it through all five senses, just being in the room. Even when under strict orders to keep his nose pressed to the knothole in the wall, he'd listened to the sounds of Willie making dinner, telling him how to peel a potato or make a gravy, doing her level best to keep his mind off his sins, talking because she liked having him there, or more likely, because she thought boys needed as much comfort as penance. He'd heard voices in the walls, made up tall tales, imagined a hundred outlaws busting through the doorway to steal Willie's good grub before they went out to rob the train. Or hang. He'd always had a certain fascination with crime and punishment.

"Your room's ready," Willie announced as she pushed a plate toward him. A plain plate except for what looked like a half pound of chocolate cake weighting it down. "I invited Josie and Justin to come out for dinner Friday night. Jeff, too, if he can get away from that hotel he insists on livin' in. I'm fixing your favorite meal, too, so don't you go tellin' me you can't stay through the weekend."

He opened his mouth to tell her he was staying until she got tired of him and kicked him out, but the words hung in his throat. The ranch belonged to Matt. No matter that the property deed stated he, Jeff and Josie were partial owners, too. The S-J was a place Alex visited, like Disneyland or New York City. A place he came back to. A place he left from. Not the place he could hang his hat. As good as it felt to be home and have Willie fuss over him, he didn't really want to be here.

He wanted to be in the run-down house next door to the Thatcher clinic. He wanted to be with Annie. "If you're making my favorite meal, Willie, I'd be plum loco not to stay, wouldn't I?"

She hovered near the table, delighted just to watch him. "Don't go givin' me your double-talk, bucko. What I want to hear is that you're flat tired of travelin' around, sleepin' in barns, eating food not fit for pig slop, and you're finally ready to settle down and stay put where you were meant to be all along."

He gave her the smile he saved just for her. "One day, Wilhemina, I'm gonna make you sorry you made that wish."

She set her hands on her hips and watched as he made a show of digging into the rich chocolate cake. "I'd sure like to see you try."

"Would you look what came in with the cat!" Matt McIntyre walked in from outside, tossed his hat onto a hatrack where it swung lazily, perfectly hooked. Just once, Alex would have liked to see that hat hit the floor, but it never did. Not even during the worst times, the years following the accident when Matt's wife and unborn baby were killed. Scooping more of the Sin-Full cake into his mouth, he watched Matt walk to the table, pull out a chair, turn it around and straddle it, facing in. "How ya doin, Tex?"

Why was it big brothers always had to remind you they were older, tougher, and smarter just in the way they asked a simple question? What was it about Matt that always had Alex feeling like a runny-nosed, cow-licked, scrawny kid? "Doing fine, Wy. Heard the one about the rancher and the dumb blonde?"

Matt grinned. "Can't say I have."

"That's because there isn't a blonde dumb enough to hook up with a rancher."

"Ha, ha. I guess it was too much trouble to pick up the phone and let us know you were heading our way?"

"Nah, it wouldn't have been any trouble at all, but I wanted it to be a surprise. You know how I hate those 'kill the fatted calf' shindigs. Besides, you knew I'd be home sometime this fall." He licked the fork and faced the moment of truth. "I bought the stallion."

Matt's eyes lit up. "Which one? The King line or the Diamond Cut?"

"Bloodline isn't everything."

"Maybe not, but it's a lot." Matt hesitated, went on, "Well, Jeff and I trust your judgment on this. You're the expert."

"Glad you feel that way. This horse is Texas born and bred, and he doesn't know his family connections are nothin' to write home about, so I don't want you telling him."

"If he can speak English, his sire must've been Mr. Ed.''

"He's out of Blue's Symphony by Polar Express and don't bother poring over your breeding charts 'cause you won't like what you find. But I promise you, Kodiak Blue speaks the language of cows as if he's part Hereford. He's entered in the Midwestern Cutting Horse futurity, and when he wins in December, our breeding program is going to hit the ground running.''

Although there was no discernible shift in posture, Matt tensed. Alex could practically feel it creep across the table toward him. "Kodiak Blue?'' Matt repeated. "Isn't that Chase Ramsey's horse? The one he shouldn't have been able to give away after last year's Congress?''

That was one way of putting it, Alex supposed. "Ramsey is a fool and he nearly ruined Koby trying to turn him into something he isn't.''

"But you're gonna turn him into a champion. Is that what you're telling me?''

The tension reached Alex, settled in like a dull headache. "Yeah, big brother. That's exactly what I'm telling you.''

"Well, now...'' Willie knew when trouble was brewing and what she could do to defuse it. "You want a piece of cake, Matt? There's plenty. How 'bout a glass of milk, Alex? Or another piece of cake for you?''

"No, thanks.'' Alex was proud of himself for holding his brother's gaze and not backing down. He was right this time, damn it. Let Matt be the one to look away. But when he finally did, Alex didn't feel much in the way of relief. ''My appetite isn't all I thought it was, Willie. Must be the excitement of being home.''

Matt shook his head to let Willie know he didn't want cake—and that there wasn't going to be a family brawl. ''What happened to your Jeep?''

''Sold it. Bought that magnificent vehicle parked outside. Didn't you see it on your way in?''

The grin returned to Matt's face, strained but passable. ''I saw it. Figured you wrecked the Jeep and were in too big a hurry to get home to replace it with a decent truck.''

''There's a damn good engine under that rusty hood.'' Alex stretched the truth a bit rather than open himself up to more criticism. ''And it's the only thing I could find big enough to haul the horse trailer I bought. Wait'll you see it.''

''If it goes with the pickup and the horse, I can only imagine.''

Had he made so many bad choices that Matt didn't believe him capable of making a right one? ''Koby didn't seem to mind it,'' he said tightly.

''So you brought the horse with you?''

''It'd be kinda hard to train him long-distance.''

''I realize that, knucklehead.'' Matt cuffed him on the shoulder, trying to restore camaraderie. ''What I'm trying to figure out is what you did with him.''

''Left the horse and the trailer at Thatcher's clinic.'' Alex pushed the plate away and Willie whisked it out of sight. "Stopped there on my way into town this afternoon."

A momentary pause criss-crossed the room, boomeranged between Matt and the housekeeper and was gone. "You stopped to see Annie?" Willie asked in a rush of curiosity she obviously couldn't stop.

"Something wrong with the horse?" Matt asked just as quickly.

"No." Alex answered both at once, then decided he might as well go ahead and explain. They'd just pester him with questions until he did. "I found an injured dog about fifty miles out and took her in to the clinic. Finding Annie there was a surprise. You'd think somebody would have told me she'd taken over old Dex's practice."

"Guess somebody thought you knew," Matt said. "You're sure there's nothing wrong with the horse?"

"Nothing a little faith and a good trainer won't cure," he offered pointedly. "Relax, Matthew. I know what I'm doing."

Matt opened his mouth to argue, but Willie got there first. "Annie's pregnant," she announced as if he might not have noticed. "She and Josie started a contest to see which baby'll be the first one born in the new century. Population around here is getting ready to boom, come January 1."

"That's what I heard." Alex sat back in the chair, relaxing again, now that he knew Matt wasn't going to kill him. Not yet, anyway. It'd been stupid to think his brother might actually have gained some faith in him over the past six months. "Josie filled me in this afternoon on the rash of expectant mothers in Bison City. Sounds like an epidemic to me."

"How many chances did she make you buy on guessing arrival times for all those babies?"

"She said I had to buy a dozen to start, but before she'd polished off Nell's cherry pie, she made me promise I'd sell a dozen more myself. Plus she said if I should guess right and win, I can't have my picture in the calendar with the New Millennium mother and baby."

"She told me the same thing," Matt agreed. "Something about us having too close a connection with the *Bugle*. Of course, if she delivers one quarter of a second after midnight December 31, I'd like to see anybody tell her her baby can't claim the prize."

Alex smiled, knowing that for the God's truth. "It's not like Josie needs to win anything. She already believes she's hit the happiness jackpot with Justin and the baby."

"I can't wait to hold that young'un in my arms," Willie said on a happy sigh.

Matt pushed up from the chair. "Looks like you better be practicing your baby talk," he said, giving Alex an affectionate, if aggressive thump on the back. "Ready or not, you're gonna be an uncle."

"I'll let you teach me everything you know about it." Alex grabbed Matt's arm as he passed and gave it a brotherly slug.

Rounding, Matt slugged back, and Alex started up out of his chair.

"Don't you start that in my kitchen," Willie warned, effectively initiating a standoff. "I swan, I don't know when you boys are gonna outgrow that roughhousing, but I'm tellin' you right now, I'm prayin' every night that this baby's a sweet little girl. Last thing we need is more McIntyre males around here."

Matt laughed.

Alex didn't. There was already another McIntyre male on the way. His son...Annie's son. Come January, Matt was going to be an uncle twice over. Providing there wasn't some misguided veterinarian-turned-carpenter over in Africa. "You ever hear of Annie being involved with some guy in the Peace Corps?" he asked with studied indifference.

"Peace Corps?" Matt repeated in much the same tone Alex had used with Annie. "She's never been in the Peace Corps. Too busy working her way through school."

"I know she's never been in the Peace Corps. I just wondered if she might be involved with some guy who is."

Willie's brow furrowed as she thought. "I never heard anything about Annie and the Peace Corps."

"Neither did I," Matt said. "What made you think that?"

Shrugging, Alex tried to look only casually interested. "She told me the father of her baby is in the Peace Corps. In Africa."

The pregnant pause returned to the kitchen with

the precision of a boomerang, then Willie and Matt spoke at once.

"Could be, I suppose."

"Possible, I guess."

Okay, so they didn't believe her story, either. He nodded as if he, too, found it plausible. "I just wondered."

"She was away at school these past few years," Willie added quickly. "She could've met him there. Just 'cause I never heard about her having any boyfriends doesn't mean she didn't have some. Well, she must've had some. She's a pretty gal, got a good head on her shoulders. Some smart guy should have snapped her right up."

Matt raised his eyebrows, obviously concurring with Willie's opinion that "some guy" hadn't been as smart as he should've been. "Truth is, Alex," he said with that big-brother-knows-best tone, "rumor has it *you're* the father of Annie's baby."

"Is that a fact?" Falling into the insouciant mannerisms of his chip-on-the-shoulder adolescence—which seemed to come back all too naturally in this kitchen—he shrugged an indifference he was far from feeling. "Well, you'd think somebody would have mentioned that to me, wouldn't you?"

"Maybe 'somebody' didn't think you'd want to know. Maybe everybody figured you'd prefer ignorance over responsibility."

Family. The people who had to take you in when you had no place else to go. The people who knew you best and loved you, anyway. The people who could cut straight to your heart in a matter of words and leave you bleeding. Times like this, Alex understood why he reverted to being a smart-ass kid in this room. He squared his shoulders and met his brother's penetrating gaze. "Then I guess there's a whole slew of somebodies who just don't know me very well."

The moment held, and again Matt was the one to look away.

"Are you sure you don't want another piece of cake?" Willie asked, her voice almost shrill with the desire to patch up the moment and make it all better again. "There's plenty here."

"Thanks, no, Willie." Matt walked to the doorway. "I'll be in my office if you need me. See you later, little brother."

Alex wanted to jump Matt, wanted to wrestle him to the ground and prove that he, too, was a grown-up. But physical force would only prove he was as immature as apparently most everyone believed he was. He always planned to walk in this room and shake hands with his brother, man to man. But somehow it never worked out that way. Somehow it always ended up with Alex on the defensive, feeling like he still had unresolved issues, something still left to prove. Arguments always seemed to end with his dad or Matt or Jeff going to the office, leaving Alex behind in the kitchen to contemplate the high cost of rebellion.

"Maybe I will have another piece of that cake," he said to Willie, knowing how to please her, at least, even though the last thing he wanted was something else to eat. "And a tall glass of milk."

She bustled about, delivering all she could in the way of comfort. "Tell me about the horse you bought," she said. "Tell me what makes him a champion."

It was more than even Annie had thought to ask.

THE FIRST THING ANNIE SAW when she stepped out of the house into the chilly October morning was the battered pickup. Suddenly there was a new spring in her steps. Well, okay, so she was more bouncy than springy these days. Still the little catch in her breath, the slight stumble in heartbeat, the quiet rush of possibility inside her made it perfectly clear she was never going to get over Alex McIntyre. She could tell herself endlessly—as she'd done most of the night—that he would never be the kind of man she needed. She could line up his sins of omission and forgive him all for a smile. She could make a list of cons a mile long and balance it with a single pro: she loved him. Even at his restless, rebellious best, she loved him. If not for the baby, she'd probably have spent last night with him instead of alone. If not for the baby, she would stroll right on out to the barn to find him this morning.

If not for the baby, she would have nothing except a lonely heart when Alex left. As he always did.

With a sigh that was as much acceptance as regret, she put her feet firmly on the path that led to the clinic.

"HE'S OUT THERE AGAIN." Genevieve had an agenda and Alex McIntyre was on it. "That's three days boarding for the horse. Four when you add in today. Plus, the dog. He was supposed to take that dog home yesterday." She made checkmarks on a clipboard, apparently keeping track of Alex's tab, if not his hours on the property. "You have to talk to him about his bill. Today."

"Okay," Annie said brightly, with no intention whatsoever of going near Alex. Today, tomorrow or next month. She'd managed to avoid him for three days and she wasn't going to willingly break that kind of record. He could owe her till Judgment Day, if that's what it took to maintain a safe distance between his good ol' cowboy charm and her silly, schoolmarm heart.

Unfortunately Genevieve didn't quite see it that way. "Don't give me that cute little 'okay.' You go out there and get a week's board from him right now. Plus what he owes for the dog." She tore a page from the clipboard and held it out to Annie. "He pays today or I turn that horse over to Sheriff Hitchcock to auction off for nonpayment of debt. Plus if he doesn't take the dog, I'm moving her out to your house, 'cause she's taking up too much kennel space in here."

Annie glanced at Loosey, who wasn't taking up any more space than Cecilia Boone's whiny Dalmatian, and was just lying in her cage with her pretty head resting on her front paws. Poor baby. Orphaned, lost, injured and now accused of "taking up space." "Loosey stays until I say she goes," Annie informed her assistant with more bravado than true backbone.

Genevieve responded with The Look—the one where she pulled her glasses halfway down her nose and frowned over the top at whoever or whatever was annoying her. Annie was pretty accustomed to it by now, even had worked out an answering smile—lifting the corners of her mouth, lips locked in a rag doll's parenthetical pleasantness. It was never easy, though, standing up to the steamroller that was Genevieve. "This clinic has always kept its charity work for those what need charity. McIntyres don't qualify."

And that, apparently, was that. Genevieve stalked from the room, leaving Annie to ponder how she could dun Alex for the money without having an actual conversation with him. If this was an ordinary clinic, with a normal employee-employer relationship, she would simply direct her employee to talk to Alex and ask him when he planned to take care of the bill. But Genevieve, who knew to the penny how much money the S-J Ranch paid yearly to the Thatcher Clinic for veterinary services rendered, didn't want to risk upsetting a McIntyre and thus had decided Annie should handle it. There were days when Annie understood why Uncle Dex was thoroughly enjoying his retirement.

When she found Alex waiting for her on her

back porch after work, she thought Genevieve might have sent him a note, demanding he talk to Annie before he left, threatening some dire consequence if he didn't. But one look at the tension in his jaw and the set of his shoulders told her something was wrong. "Can you take a look at Koby?" he asked without preamble. "He's pulled up lame. I'm afraid it's something serious."

Annie turned on her heel and headed for the barn, knowing that if Koby had an injury of any magnitude, Alex's dream of winning the December futurity was worse than dead. He'd have to start over with another horse. It might take years before the S-J breeding program got off the ground. "Which leg? When did it happen?"

"Front left. Noticed it when I was bringing him in. I've been working him with your uncle's cattle. Dex said it was okay. I've been meaning to come by and talk to you about leaving Koby here instead of taking him out to the ranch. Your facilities are better, and frankly there's a lot less...distraction."

"For you or the horse?" she asked, knowing the dilemma without even having to think about it. Alex didn't want Matt supervising Koby's training, no matter how peripherally, no matter how well intentioned.

"Both."

"Too many opinions at the ranch, huh?"

"Something like that, yeah." He was ahead of her then, leading the way to the stall where Koby was calmly crunching hay. "Careful, he's a little touchy about that leg."

"I think I know how to handle myself around a horse, Alex." It was just long-legged cowboys who caused her trouble. Patting Koby's neck, she soothed him with her voice as she eased in beside him and slid her hands down his leg in a preliminary examination. The fetlock was warm to the touch and she instantly felt the puffiness of some low-grade swelling. When she applied a light pressure, Koby flinched. Lifting his foot, she duplicated her efforts, then watched his response when he again placed his weight on the leg. "Bowed tendon," she said.

"You sure?"

Straightening slowly—as much because of her own bulky condition than her desire to be thorough—she ran an assessing eye over the horse's shoulders and back, noted his calm demeanor, the way he went right back to eating without any sign of discomfort, before letting her gaze return to the fetlock. "Positive."

"That's good, then," he said, but she heard the discouragement in his voice, saw it in the taut set of his shoulders. "How long will he be out of commission?"

Annie knew Alex knew the answer to that. He'd spent his life around horses, had probably seen more bowed tendons than she'd treated in her brief career. But knowing the injury was minor didn't lessen the impact of losing a month's training time. Maybe more.

"It could be a lot worse. With a mild strain like this, you may be able to start him on an easy training schedule by the end of the month. He needs stall rest for a few days, then next week we can try him with ten, fifteen minutes of hand walking. The next week, if we're lucky, he may be able to handle five to ten minutes a day on the lunge line. After that we'll have to see how it goes.''

He slipped his hands in his hip pockets and nodded, although without much enthusiasm.

''I can get one of the high school boys who help around the clinic to exercise him, if you want,'' she offered.

''I think I know how to exercise my own horse, Annie.''

His voice reflected the stress he was under, and she wanted to make him feel better. ''I didn't mean to imply you didn't. Or that you wouldn't want to. I'm just saying if you need help, it's available.''

''Yeah, well, what I need is for this not to have happened.''

''But of all the things that could have gone wrong, Alex, this really isn't so bad.''

''When anything goes wrong with this horse, it's bad. I've staked everything on him, Annie. Everything.''

She didn't know what more reassurance she could offer. Or even if she should try. ''A few days away from cows and cowboys will probably fix him right up. So stop worrying about it, okay?''

He pushed back his hat, stroked Koby with genuine affection, absolute concern, and told Annie by his silence that he'd invested more than he should have in one contest, one horse. ''Listen,'' she said impulsively. "Could you maybe come up to the house, give me a hand with that paintbrush tonight? Maybe throw together some kind of supper?"

Way to go, Annie. You avoid the man all week, then invite him in to supper and a paint job because his horse is hurt and he's upset and you want to make him feel better? What is wrong with you, anyway?

He didn't answer for a minute. Just gave Koby a final pat and closed up the stall. Not until she turned to leave, feeling shut out and helpless, did he speak. "What happened? You run out of frozen pizza?"

"Forget it," she said, wishing she hadn't even made the effort. "I'll do the painting myself."

"Annie..." He caught her hand as she turned to go and, in typical Alex style, pulled her into a kiss she had no clue was coming. Without so much as a split second of hesitation, his lips closed over hers, firm, demanding, familiar...oh, so familiar...and knowing. Oh, but he knew her so well. How else could one kiss be all she'd remembered it to be, everything she needed it to be? In an instant of tactile sensation, she forgot the rest of her good intentions, the whole kit and caboodle of reasons to stay away from him. Her skin went warm all over, her heart beat like a frantic bird. She couldn't breathe, couldn't think, couldn't let go...and then the baby kicked. Hard, and several times in a row, as if in protest.

The baby, she thought.

"The baby," he said, pulling back abruptly, staring at her rounded belly. "He...did he kick me?"

Annie stepped back, putting some protective space between herself and the father of her son. "I don't think it was personal," she said, striving for a light, no-big-deal tone. "He just likes to move around."

"I know the feeling." Without shifting his gaze, Alex extended his hand, palm out, hovering a couple of inches from her stomach. He hesitated, raised his eyes to meet hers. "Can I— Do you mind if I—"

Okay, so she had no conviction, no strength of resolve, no willpower where he was concerned. "No," she said softly. "I don't mind." Then, sliding her hand around his, she pressed his palm against the cotton of her smock, settling it where she'd last felt the baby's kick. Looking at the span of his fingers, feeling the warmth radiating outward from his touch, hearing the uneven and unnaturally quiet sound of his breathing—as if any noise would upset the fragile balance—tenderness flooded her in a fierce rush. Sharing. This was what the word meant, she realized. This was how a family was born. Not the moment of conception. Not the moment the baby took his first, wobbly breath. Moments like this—with three hearts willing, wanting and waiting to share the kick of new life.

Chapter Five

"It's not like he does it on cue," Annie said while she painted the windowsill in the second bedroom, soon-to-be nursery. "Some days he doesn't kick at all."

Alex plunged the roller into the pan of Rodeo Tan paint and let it get a good soaking before he slapped it back onto the wall. "So you've told me about a hundred times just since supper."

"I've said it twice and I only mentioned it again because you don't act as if you believe me."

"Annie, for Pete's sake. It's a baby, not a trick rabbit. I know you can't make him kick if he doesn't want to." Alex wished she'd stop trying to make him feel better. The truth was Koby had a bowed tendon and the baby hadn't made a move after those initial Hey!-quit-pressuring-me kicks. The day hadn't exactly ended on a high note, and he'd just as soon not talk about it anymore. It was bad enough he'd stood in the barn with his palm pressed to Annie's pregnant belly, waiting for a baby she said wasn't even his to do a round of calisthenics. He'd waited until his and Annie's hands were sweaty from the contact, until the tension shifted from sweet to funny to flat-out awkward, until she apologetically withdrew from the touch. It had been her withdrawal that bothered him the most, for some obscure reason. Maybe because he'd just kissed her. Maybe because he wanted so much to feel connected to the child she carried. Maybe because he simply needed to know he belonged somewhere.

But the baby hadn't kicked, Annie had pulled away, and the moment had passed. At least it would if she'd stop talking about it.

"I just didn't want you to feel bad," she said, making him feel worse by not dropping the subject altogether.

"I feel fine, Annie. Next time the baby kicks, I'll be there to feel it for sure. Now, look at this wall and tell me if it needs a second coat."

She turned away from the window—Daffodil Yellow dripping from her trim brush onto the plastic drop cloth—and eyed the Rodeo Tan wall. She squinted, turned her head, squinted some more. "I don't know. I'm not sure I like this color combination. It looked different in the store."

"It'll look lighter when it's dry," he commented, hoping she wasn't about to change her mind.

"Josie's going to come over and stencil a border around the window frame and along the top of the wall. Animal shapes, I think." Annie frowned at the fresh paint. "I just don't know about this color."

"The colors are nice, gives the room a kind of Southwestern flavor. I like this a whole lot better than an unimaginative pastel."

"You're just saying that because you don't want to have to repaint it."

Abso-damn-lutely true. "The room's not that big, Annie. I could repaint it in a couple of hours. Maybe less." He didn't want to, but he could. "If you don't like Rodeo Tan and Daffodil, it can be Ocean Blue and Tangerine by this time tomorrow."

"Ocean Blue and Tangerine," she repeated as if considering the combination. "That would make me sick."

"Like seasick?"

"No, like orange walls and blue trim. Yuck."

He hadn't thought it sounded that bad. "I was thinking more of orange trim and blue walls."

She frowned at him and proceeded to stretch, sticking out her basketball of a belly as she kneaded the muscles in her back. He would have liked to rub her back for her, to lay aside the paint roller, walk over and thoroughly massage the sleek, fair skin beneath her oversize shirt. But she was already skittish of his touch, regretful she'd allowed their earlier embrace, and he knew if he offered she'd only make some joking excuse. But a rejection, however nicely phrased, was still a rejection. So he just watched her stretch and pretended his thoughts were focused on painting. "I 'spose we could go with a nice Grass Green and Plum Purple combo," he said.

She straightened even as she wrinkled her cute little nose in distaste. "On second thought, I like this color combination just fine."

"Good choice." He returned to work, happily imagining how much pleasure he'd get from throwing this cheap excuse for a paint roller in the trash. "The boy will thank you once he learns to talk."

"The boy?"

"The baby. You said it's a boy."

"Oh, right. The baby." She nodded, as if the thought was distracting. "I've been calling him Sam. What do you think?"

Sam. My son, Sam. "I like that a lot. It was my great-grandfather's name, you know. Samuel."

"Oh." Annie turned away abruptly. "Well, I haven't decided for sure. It was just a thought." She was talking too fast, as if she'd just realized that naming the baby after one of Alex's ancestors might not be so smart. Especially if she wanted Alex to go on believing he wasn't the dad. "I also like the name Hoyt."

Not in this lifetime, Alex thought. Don't worry, kid, I'll save you from that one. "Hoyt. Now there's a solid name for you. Of course, you'd have to make sure the first name fits with the last. A kid can't grow up being called Hoyt Foyt, for instance. Or Hoyt Faloy. Same thing with Rudy. Sounds okay with a last name like Jones or Miller. Not so great if he's going by Rudy Tooten."

She fought a smile. He could see the twitch at the corners of her lips. "I can see I'll have to give this some more thought." She settled herself on a small stool and went to work on the bottom sill, finishing the yellow trim.

Alex considered the matter and decided her smile was worth pursuing, especially since he hadn't seen much of it all evening. She was jumpier than usual, too, and he knew it was because he'd kissed her in the barn. That kiss had been the single, nicest part of his entire day and, unless he was reading her wrong, she was flat-out determined to pretend it had never even happened. She didn't want him to kiss her—or at least she didn't want him to think it meant anything to her if he did—and she didn't want him to be the father of her baby, even if he was. She avoided him for three days, then asked him over to share her supper and an evening of painting the nursery—because she didn't want him to feel bad.

Women. They could turn a man crazier than a bug in a bedroll. Well, truth was, he didn't know about most women. He only knew about Annie. He rolled paint to within an inch of the ceiling and brought the roller back at a slant. "I've always been partial to Sundance myself."

"The film festival?"

"No, the Kid. You know, Butch Cassidy and the Sundance Kid. When I was about ten, I wanted to change my name to Sundance."

She laughed aloud—an unexpected bonus. "I remember that," she said. "You came to school after Christmas break that year, wearing your brand-new, Cowboy Carl Six-Shooter and Holster play set, and told the teacher—what was her name?—Carter. That's it. You told Mrs. Carter that Captain Kidd was your great-great-grandpappy and you weren't answering to anything but Sundance Kid or, for short, 'The Kid.'"

He laughed, too. "I forgot about that. I never could persuade Mrs. Carter, or the principal, to call me anything but trouble."

"You were always such a rebel, Alex. I hope this baby doesn't—"

The sentence broke apart suddenly and he filled in the blank. "Inherit my renegade spirit?"

"Ha!" It was supposed to be an incredulous sound, supporting the impossibility of his erroneous assumption. In Alex's opinion, it fell far short of the target.

"I was going to say something entirely different." She grabbed a wet rag and scrubbed furiously at a fresh Daffodil Yellow mark on the Rodeo Tan wall. "This seems to be a difficult concept for you, Alex, but this is my baby and he couldn't have inherited so much as an eyelash from your gene pool. He's going to be a Thatcher, through and through."

Alex came close with the roller and rolled a swatch of paint over the spot she'd just streaked into a wide blemish. "What? No humanitarian tendencies? No talent for carpentry? No characteristics handed down from dear old dad?"

She looked up, eyes wary, frown well-situated

on her lips. Lips he badly wanted to kiss again. "You're making fun of a very important person in my life, Alex, and I want you to stop it right now."

"Imaginary" person was more accurate, but he couldn't very well argue the point with her. He couldn't very well kiss her again, either. He wanted to do both, but had enough sense—momentarily—not to. He actually meant to back off then, give her a little space, show her he was mature enough to let her have the last word this time, but fate intervened in the form of a drip. Rodeo Tan. Right between her pretty green eyes.

Uh-oh, he thought. "Woops," he said.

She brought the rag to her forehead in automatic response and smeared the drop into a blaze of war paint. Then she reached out with her brush and swiped a stripe across the scuffed toes of his boots. A Daffodil Yellow stripe. Bringing her gaze to his, she shrugged. "Woops."

Looking from the paint on his boots to the paint on her face, he gave the roller a stiff shake and splattered her with fine droplets of Rodeo Tan. "Never," he drawled, "paint a cowboy's boots."

"Oh, yeah?" With cool deliberation, she slid her finger across the end of her brush, spattering polka dots around the stripe that crossed the toe of each leather boot. "Who says? Miss Manners?"

He gave the roller another shake, flecking her in a more uniform coverage. "It's not in some sissy book, Calamity Ann. It's the law."

"The law of averages?"

She was a sitting duck as far as he was concerned, but he kept his eye on her all the same. "The law of the West," he told her. "And that supercedes any rules of etiquette made up in this century."

"Big words for a man wearing yellow boots."

She was not playing fair, being so sassy and flirty just when he'd been ready to back off and be mature. "Maybe," he conceded. "But not for a man holding a paint roller over your head."

"I'm not afraid of you. I'm 100 percent washable."

Now, there was a pleasantly distracting idea. "I suppose you expect me to paint you up, then strip you down and give you a good scrubbin' afterward. Maybe a nice back rub."

"In your dreams, McIntyre. In…your… dreams." She pushed up from the stool. At least, she tried. Her balance was a little off center, though, and she sat down again with a plop. Sighing, she frowned at him. "You're going to have to give me a hand up, so I can stalk out of here indignantly."

He grinned. "There was a time in my life when I'd've been right happy to lend a hand toward seeing a sight like that. Unfortunately for you, I've seen women stalk away indignantly more times than I care to recall. It's not such an amusing diversion anymore."

"Considering how many times I've watched you stalk off, I think you owe me a hand up."

He held the paint roller like a shepherd's staff, leaning lazily toward her. "Come on, Annie, you know I never stalked anywhere in my life, especially not away from you.''

"However you did it, Alex, it was always me who was left behind, wasn't it?''

True enough, but not nearly complicated enough to be the whole truth, either. "Fact remains, you're sittin' and I'm standin' and if you want my help, you're gonna have to offer a little trade.''

She struggled to push up again, but he stayed carefully in her way, so she couldn't quite get her center of gravity shifted. It was either take his hand or set hers on the freshly painted windowsill. "You can have anything except my firstborn," she said. "And a few other things.''

"All I want is to know why you've been avoiding me all week.''

"Good sense?'' she suggested.

"That's never stopped you before.''

"I finally worked my way though college. Came out smarter, especially when it comes to you.''

"That would explain why I'm painting this room for you, I guess.''

She smiled, making his knees go nearly as wobbly as a newborn foal's. "You're doing the painting because I felt sorry for you this afternoon. Thought you needed something to take your mind off your horse.''

She always understood, even when he'd just as soon she didn't. "You ought to know better than to come between a cowboy and his melancholy.'' He laid the paint roller on the floor and squatted down in front of her, bringing them toe-to-toe and face-to-face. "Koby's going to be right as rain in a couple of weeks. You said so yourself."

"A month," she cautioned. "Nothing but stall rest and light exercise for a month. You don't want to make things worse."

He looked into her eyes and tried to convey the sincerity he felt. "Making things worse is the last thing I want to do, Annie. For Koby…or for you."

He watched her expression soften with wistful longing, a longing quickly tempered by the memories of past disappointments. "No need to worry about that," she said in an overly bright, overly flippant tone. "The only way you could make things worse for me is to show up tomorrow with cans of orange and blue paint. Or any other dreadful combination."

Okay, so she wasn't ready to forgive him for all the times he'd let her down. He could understand that. He could deal with that. Changing her mind had always been a challenge, one he often savored. Straightening, he offered her a strictly friendly hand up. "I promise you this room will remain Rodeo Tan and Daffodil Yellow, as long as I have anything to say about it. Believe it or not, I'm actually not all that fond of painting—even when my horse is lame and I don't have anything better to do."

She smiled, not easily, but she didn't expend a whole lot of effort on it, either. "I'm sure Matt will have plenty of work for you to do at the ranch. The time Koby's out of training will fly by."

Whether it was the mention of Matt or just pure

inspiration on his part, Alex suddenly realized he had a month to get Annie situated. It wasn't that he minded ranch work, but he wasn't crazy about working for his oldest brother. Once Koby won the cutting futurity and the breeding and training programs were established, Alex would be able to work at the ranch on his own terms. He'd have his own niche, his own schedule. Free and clear of Matt's supervision. Well, mostly free and clear. But for now, while he was still unproven, still the irresponsible, pie-in-the-sky-eyed little brother, he'd much prefer to keep his distance from the ranch.

His time would be better spent helping Annie. In a month he could have this house fixed up and ready for the baby. He could have Annie eating nutritious meals, instead of frozen pizza. He could repair the sink, put in a dishwasher, close in that back room, improve the place, generally make life easier for her. God knew she needed someone to do it. In a month's time, he could show her he was responsible, capable, dependable—all those "able" qualities she'd always admired in his brothers. Surely in a month of days...and nights...he could prove to her that he had sense enough to know and appreciate the important things in life. "I expect you'll be seeing me around," he said, picking up the paint bucket and brushes. "A cowboy doesn't like to be separated from his horse, you know."

"Starting tonight, you'll have Loosey to keep you company."

Lucy?

"She's such a sweetheart, Alex...and loves to plant slurpy kisses on anyone who shows her the least bit of attention."

"Well, then, I'm sure looking forward to meeting her."

Annie rolled her eyes. "Loosey is your dog," she explained. "Footloose. Remember? We'll go up to the clinic and spring her as soon as we've finished cleaning up."

The dog. He'd forgotten all about the dog. "Great," he said with completely false enthusiasm. What was he going to do with a dog? Willie had never been crazy about having pets in the house and he had a suspicion Annie wouldn't be crazy about the idea of turning a dog with a broken leg loose on the ranch. Maybe he could convince Josie to take it, although he was pretty sure Annie wouldn't think much of that solution, either.

"I'll go over the medications with you," Annie continued, either oblivious of or unconcerned about his dilemma. "It's very important she takes all of the meds. Plus, she's going to need some exercise, too."

"I'll tie her to Koby's lead and let them walk each other." He saw her lips tighten and added a hasty, "Just kidding."

While she undoubtedly knew he was joking, she also had to know that no matter how cheery his tone or how quick his grin, he did not want the shepherd-collie or any other pet.

"You hit the dog, Alex, it's only fair you take care of her—at least until she's well."

"I didn't hit her," he said, wondering why it was so hard to believe he hadn't been speeding, hadn't been careless, hadn't hit the stupid dog. "I stopped to help her after she got hit by someone else."

Annie turned toward the door. "Then you're her Good Samaritan, which means you still get to take care of her until she recovers."

"I never said I wouldn't."

"Good. Genevieve has your bill ready, too. She handed it to me as she was going out the door this evening, with the advice that I get a check before you up and left."

"Are you worried I'll skip town without paying the bill?"

She frowned at him, surprised perhaps by the irritation in the words. "No, I'm not. Genevieve is. But then, she suspects anyone who doesn't pay in advance of being a deadbeat pet owner."

"What about you, Annie? What do you think?"

"I'm not worried about the money."

"But you're convinced I'd be a deadbeat dad?"

She met his gaze, truthfully. "I believe you'd have the best intentions in the world, Alex." Then, with a sigh, she shrugged away the sudden seriousness. "Who knows? By the time you meet and marry the right woman, maybe you'll be ready to make some lucky little boy a terrific dad. In the meantime, you can practice on your niece or nephew."

He couldn't remember being really angry with her. Ever. Until now. "I intend to be a part of my son's life, Annie, whether you have any faith in me or not."

"It's not a matter of fai—"

"The hell it isn't!" He stopped, forced his lungs to expand, exhale…slow down, calm down, take a moment. "It is, Annie. It is about having faith."

She pressed her lips together, stood so still, looked so vulnerable that for a second he thought she might toss caution to the wind and believe him. Or that she at least wanted to. "This isn't about you, Alex. It's not even your—"

"If you're about to tell me again that this isn't my baby, don't bother, because no matter how many times you tell me, I'm not going to believe you."

"Well, that would make this a draw, I guess. I don't believe you. You don't believe me. So here's what we're going to do. I'm putting my six-shooter away and you're going to do the same. No gunfight today. Because sure as we're standing here, if we keep arguing, one of us is bound to get hurt and I'm too tired to feel guilty or regretful tonight." She wiped her palms on the sides of her shirt. "Now I'm going to go get your bill and you can write out a check to the clinic, which will make Genevieve happy. Then we'll go retrieve your dog, which will make Loosey happy. After that you're going home and I'm going to wash this paint off and go to bed, which will make me happy. Any questions?"

Here's your hat, what's your hurry, and a noticeable nonmention of what would make him happy. Alex picked up the roller pan and poured the remaining paint into the bucket, not sure if he even wanted the option of arguing his case right now. Okay, so maybe he'd pushed too hard. Maybe he'd wanted too much, too fast. But Annie, of all people, should know she could depend on him when there was a child at stake. He straightened slowly, looked around for the lid to the paint can. "I'll pay Koby's board through October," he said tightly. "Wouldn't want anyone stayin' awake and worryin' over whether I'll be around at the end of the month."

"Genevieve wouldn't miss a night's sleep over you, Alex, believe me. She'd insist I do it."

The little catch in Annie's voice told him she didn't want him to be angry or upset. But the glint of determination in her eyes assured him she wasn't backing down, either. She didn't believe he could stick around long enough to make much of a father…or a husband. Hell, maybe she was right. "I don't want you losing a wink of your beauty rest over me, darlin'," he said. "I'll pay two months ahead if that's what it takes."

"No need to get carried away. You'll be itching to move Koby out of here by that time. And Genevieve will be thrilled with a whole month's stall rent. She might even start speaking to you again."

Alex offered a smile—a poor excuse for one, perhaps, but still a smile. "On second thought, maybe I'll pay week to week."

Annie's answering grin was worth the effort. She moved—a bit stiffly, he thought—to the doorway and looked back at the room. "I believe Hoyt is going to like his room," she said.

Alex turned from watching her to the warm color on the walls, the sunny shade of the trim, and a slow-building panic at the thought of the baby whose presence would soon fill every nook and cranny of Annie's world. "Yep. The Sundance Kid is going to be very happy here." He looked to the doorway in hopes of sharing both the panic and the anticipation of parenthood.

But she was already gone.

LOOSEY TOOK ONE CAUTIOUS, skeptical sniff of Alex's outstretched hand and fell all over herself with excitement. Here was her rescuer, her savior, her hero. Her plume of a tail, freshly bathed and groomed along with the scrawny rest of her, wagged like the white flag of surrender. Her tongue, rough, pink, and wet, slapped kisses on his hands, his arms, his knees, his face, everywhere he allowed her to reach. Her eyes shone with the adoration in her doggy heart. She might have one neon blue leg cast, but it was clear her gratitude was pure-white and knew no encumbrance. With one rescue, Alex had won her heart until the end of time.

Annie understood completely…and as she watched the dog's zealous affection and Alex's more measured response, she felt a strong dose of sympathy for them both. Loosey, because there would always be hope, but never a promise that she'd be allowed to stay with him. Alex, because he could have had so much love just for the taking…if he hadn't been so intent on proving he was good enough, worthy enough to receive it.

After they left, driving off in the decrepit old pickup, the man and his newly acquired companion, Annie wandered back to the baby's room to lean against the door frame and survey the empty nursery. The paint was drying lighter, as Alex had predicted, and the walls were turning a warm, rusty-tan, brightened by the pale yellow trim. The colors reminded her of something—a pleasurable something—and as she tried to remember what, the child in her womb kicked once, then again, then with a rolling, energetic frequency. "Oh, sure," she said to him. "*Now* you're going to show off."

But it was probably best that Alex hadn't felt the baby kick, that there had been no opportunity for father and fetus to bond, that a moment when the three of them might have forged family ties had slipped away unsung. It didn't matter if this baby wound up being Sam or Sundance or Billy, his name would sound right with Thatcher. Not McIntyre. She didn't care if Alex or his entire family was convinced her son belonged in part to them, this child was hers to protect. This was her baby and hers alone. She had determined early on she would be both mother and father to her boy and she was sticking to that promise. No matter how many flat-out lies she had to tell. No matter who did or didn't believe her. It was her own foolish fault if she allowed Alex to break her heart. It was inexcusable to allow him any chance at all of breaking her son's.

Her hand reached to switch off the bedroom light, the shy memory pounced, and she found herself thinking about the kitten Alex had given her one long-ago autumn. The runt of the litter, Boots, was barely a half pound of rusty-colored fur, dotted with black eyes and a pink nose, with front paws capped in mottled white. Alex had rescued the little guy from certain starvation—when the mother cat had rejected him in favor of his plentiful, more robust littermates—and brought him to Annie, who'd nursed him to health with an eyedropper and the sheer power of love.

Boots had been her first real patient, her first knowledge of vocation, her first true glimpse into the exceedingly sweet tenderness in Alex's then thirteen-and-gawky teenage heart. It hadn't been his fault Boots died a few weeks later. It was just one of those things. Uncle Dex said it wasn't always a kindness to save the runt, but Annie hadn't believed him then. Or even now, when she understood that technically, medically speaking his statement had some basis in fact.

Alex had taken the kitten's death hard, blamed himself somehow, even though he'd denied he cared one way or another. When she'd said she wanted to give Boots a proper funeral, Alex had made no bones about his opinion. It was just a silly cat, he'd said. She'd hoped he would change his mind, show up at the designated time, put his arm around her shoulders while she cried for that small, silly, sweet cat. But he hadn't…and she'd held the graveside service by herself in Uncle Dexter's pasture.

Annie flipped the switch, cloaking the rusty-tan walls in nothing but moonlight, but still she lingered in the doorway. Boots had had a funny, half squawk, half meow that sounded more like a bluejay than a barn cat. He'd slept on her pillow, played tirelessly with her hair, drunk from the faucet and loved her with all his small might. And when she'd gone back the following spring to try to find his grave, she'd discovered that someone had marked it with a polished stone and scattered wildflower seeds. Seeds that had bloomed into a sunny blanket of soft, pale yellow all around Boots's grave.

There were times, Annie thought as she turned away, when she could forgive Alex anything.

Chapter Six

Alex hadn't driven a mile before Loosey had wedged herself against his side like a pesky cocklebur. Another mile had her muzzle and the uninjured front paw on his thigh. Two miles more and she'd managed to wriggle most of her body across his lap, squeezing into the open space between him and the steering wheel. At this rate, by the time he reached the S-J gates, the silly mutt would be driving.

He didn't know why he didn't just stop the truck and forcibly put her back on her side of the seat. Most dogs would have stuck their nose through the window he'd rolled down a few inches for that very purpose. But Loosey wasn't interested in the night scents outside or in sniffing out where she was headed. She was only concerned about getting as close to him as he and the logistics of the pickup truck would permit.

"You're trespassin' on my good nature, Footloose," Alex said, absently brushing his hand across her black-and-tan fur. "What kind of name is that for a dog, anyway? I'll bet Annie made it up just to see if she could set my hat to spinnin'. Which explains how she could come up with a name like Hoyt for a baby.''

Loosey's tail flopped against the cracked vinyl seat covers, acknowledging the sound of his voice, if not her agreement.

"I ask you, Loose, don't you think Sundance has Hoyt beat all to pieces when it comes to naming a boy?''

Again, the *thump, thump* of her approval.

"Me, too." Alex draped his hand over the wheel, at home as long as he was on the move. "Who ever heard of anything ever being named after Hoyt? Sundance. Now there's a name for you. Got an outlaw, a film festival, a catalog and at least one ski resort named Sundance. 'Course, I'm not really meanin' I want to name my son after an outlaw or a catalog, you understand. If it was left to me, I'd probably settle on Sam. But it'd be nice to have some say-so, don't ya think?''

Loosey apparently thought so, too, because she wiggled her hips and gained another inch of lap, all but taking over the driver's seat.

"Scoot over," he said, shifting her hind legs back onto the seat and getting a little room to drive. "We may as well get a few things straight right up-front, pooch. First off, you're no lapdog. Second, if Annie hadn't taken a shine to you, and if she hadn't got the notion it'd be good for me to have to take care of you, you'd be out there thumbing a ride—which is what got you into this predicament in the first place. So no matter what anybody else tells you, you're lucky to have me, understand?''

Loosey licked his sleeve.

"Third and most important, I wasn't lookin' for a pet when I found you, so don't go gettin' any ideas on that score. Where I grew up and where we're headed, animals serve a useful purpose or they don't stick around. Get the picture? Josie was always trying to sneak kittens in from the barn, but Willie caught her every time. The thing about dogs, you see, is they're harder to sneak in and a lot harder to hide. Believe me, I know. Willie likes animals, don't get me wrong. She just doesn't think they belong in the house. Now I'm willing to sneak you in, but after that, it's gonna be up to you to keep a low profile, if you know what I mean.'' Alex looked down at the dog in his lap, realized he was rubbing the silky underside of her ear, an action she seemed real happy about. "Willie catches you and you're on your own. Got it?''

Loosey closed her eyes and sighed happily, apparently convinced that as long as she could get him to scratch her ear, she could take on the world.

"What am I doing talking to you?'' he asked, although he knew the answer. There wasn't anyone else to listen to him. He hadn't exactly spent his life talking out his problems with other people. "All you care about is having something to eat and a place to sleep and gettin' your ear scratched. You don't care that my horse pulled a tendon today or that if he's not ready for the futurity, my whole future goes sprintin' off like a wolf after a rabbit. You certainly don't care I'm about to become a father, and the mother of my baby can't locate enough faith in me to even admit I had something to do with it.''

Loosey looked at him as if she did care, as if she did understand.

"Yeah, well, I've been fooled by that soulful look in a female's eyes before,'' he told her. "You're going to have to do something pretty spectacular if you want me to believe you're concerned about anything other than getting your ears rubbed.''

She barked. Once. Like Lassie, only not so energetically.

"Sure. Sure. I hear you. But what's that supposed to mean? That you understand? Ha.''

The singular syllable reminded him of Annie, of the way she'd scoffed at the idea her baby might take after him. What was she thinking, anyway, making up some imaginary guy to be the baby's father? The smart thing for her to do would be to claim Alex as the father—whether he was or not— and marry him. The McIntyre name wasn't anything to sneeze at—even if it didn't go well with Hoyt. And while he knew marriage to him might not be a picnic, he sure didn't believe it would be a lifetime in purgatory, either.

She was just being stubborn, he decided. Paying him back for all the times he hadn't been there when she'd wanted him. He would admit he hadn't always been Johnny-on-the-spot. He'd messed up a few times—times when it counted. He deserved some tough negotiations to earn her forgiveness. That part he knew. What he didn't understand was her denial. Flat, uncompromising denial. Was it possible the baby wasn't his?

But it had to be. The timing was all wrong, otherwise. He knew Annie Thatcher the same way he knew the geography of northern Wyoming. He knew she wouldn't have spent one night with him and the next with another man. It wasn't in her nature. Lying to him for what she considered a good cause? Yes. Hopping from one bed to another in the space of a week? No. Definitely no.

Plus he'd seen no sign, nothing to indicate the presence of another man in Annie's life. No pictures lying around, no postcards or gifts from faraway places, no soft, wistful sighs, no dreamy look in her eyes, no sense that there was—or ever had been—anyone else. No matter what she said, the facts didn't add up to another man. She wouldn't admit the baby was his because she didn't want him in her life. Hard as that was to swallow, he couldn't figure out any other plausible explanation.

Annie had been mad at him more times than he could recall over the years. Often, with good reason. But he just couldn't believe he'd ever done anything so terrible she'd feel she needed to protect his son from him. It was true he'd missed some important events in her life. Sometimes for no better reason than he believed she'd be better off without him. But at worst his sins were of the omission variety, not of the irreparable-damage sort. Certainly nothing to have given her the idea he would be such a terrible father that any child was bound to suffer for his influence.

So was she protecting his son? Or protecting herself?

Either way, Alex had to change her mind. Had to prove he wasn't the risk she apparently believed him to be. Which was more than she would have asked of any other man. "Why do I have to prove anything?" he asked aloud, causing Loosey to freeze her persistent inching onto his lap and look up at him. "And don't even think about taking her side in this," he instructed the dog, although he knew that on this topic, there was probably no one who would line up to support his cause.

Why should he be surprised about that, either? He'd rebelled against authority and expectations since childhood. Maybe he hadn't been born the natural athlete Matt was, and maybe he'd never been as book smart as Jeff…or maybe he'd never been able to figure out just why he should put out the effort. Teachers complained he didn't apply himself to schoolwork. His parents complained he didn't apply himself to ranch work. His brothers complained his escapades got them in trouble. Whatever the demand on his time and energies, Alex had had to find a way to complicate it—either to keep from being bored or merely for the attention value.

His parents were hardworking, goal-oriented, practical individuals who took great pride in their children's accomplishments and didn't know what to make of Alex's restless need to push the boundaries, probe the limits, explore the possibilities. His too-tender heart had toughened up early under the two-against-one teasing Matt and Jeff delivered in their shared role of big brother. His achievements were always overshadowed by one of theirs, often even by Josie's little-girl-cute antics. Alex would be the first to admit he hadn't been an easy child, but then, how could he have known the difference between easy and difficult if he hadn't been told again and again?

A little more trust and a little less criticism would have been nice. On the other hand, maybe he had—as Willie had once said—been born on the cusp of the new moon and just never quite got his life's bearings. Whatever the reason for his skittish nature, it was time to pay the piper.

Because no matter what any of them expected, he was home, and home he was going to stay. Where else did a man belong except in the place his heart had always resided? Annie would see. He'd show her he was a handy man to have around. He'd show Matt and Jeff that he knew more about cutting horses than they'd ever learn. And he'd prove to them all that he was man enough to be a good father to his son.

After all, he had nearly three whole months before the futurity.

Three months before the baby was due.

Three months before he had to decide what happened if somehow proving himself a man turned out to be more task than he was equal to.

JEFF'S CAR PARKED near the house was hardly an unusual sight at the S-J. Alex didn't think much about it—just wondered what had brought his brother to the ranch and what had kept him so late at night. It was past ten when Alex walked in through the back door and tossed his hat toward the rack, where it missed a hook and swan-dived to the floor. Picking it up, he set it square on the peg, then turned to explore what might have been left over from dinner. It wasn't until he pulled back the aluminum foil on the plate Willie had left warming in the oven that he realized the day, Friday, and the import of his favorite dish, stuffed pork chops and stewed apples, neatly packed in the divided sections of the warming tray. Tonight was the party Willie had planned for the family, the dinner she'd made especially for him.

Disappointment sluiced through him and settled into a sick feeling in his gut. How could he have forgotten something so important? And how would he ever be able to make it up to Willie?

"You're a little late for dinner," Jeff observed as he walked in from the other part of the house. "We waited until eight for you to show up, but…" His voice faded and he gave a little whistle of surprise as he caught a glimpse of the skinny dog hobbling along behind Alex's every move. "You are living dangerously tonight, little brother."

Alex leaned down to pat Loosey on the head, hoping to keep at least one someone on his side. "I thought I might be able to slip her in without

Willie noticing. I can't leave her outside. Her leg's broken."

"You may be in similar circumstances unless you steer clear of Matt for a few days. He's a tad riled that you missed dinner."

"I forgot," Alex said simply, feeling like the worst kind of heel. No wonder they all had such low expectations of him. He delivered inexcusable behavior like clockwork. "I had a lot of things on my mind this evening—what with Koby and Annie and all—and I just plain forgot about Willie's little get-together."

"Koby?" Jeff questioned, then provided his own answer. "Oh, yes. Kodiak Blue. The horse that's going to put the S-J breeding and training project on the map. Matt's a tad riled about that, too."

"Matt was raised on sour milk. At least, when it comes to anything I do."

Jeff's shrug could have been agreement or simple understanding. "He expects you to listen to him, instead of going off half-cocked to do the exact opposite of any advice he's seen fit to give you. I admit I'm a little puzzled about this particular decision myself. I thought the three of us agreed you'd choose breeding stock from the list Matt put together. You know how he feels about bloodlines, yet after six months with barely any word at all, you suddenly show up with maybe the one horse in the whole damn country guaranteed to send Matt's blood pressure soaring higher than the Tetons. You've made it damned hard to defend you, 'Lex.''

"I don't need your defense, Jeff. Koby is a good horse. A great horse. He's going to win the cutting futurity regardless of how little faith you, Matt, or anyone else has in him. He's going to win because he's got something more important than blue blood. He's got the heart of a champion and the spirit of a competitor. He will win, Jeff. He will." Alex met his brother's doubt with resolution. "He'll win hands down…providing he makes a complete recovery."

"Recovery?"

"Bowed tendon. Happened this evening."

Jeff hid his dismay, but not so well that Alex didn't see it anyway. "No wonder you forgot about dinner," Jeff said. "What happened?"

"I don't know. He just pulled up lame as we were heading back to the barn. I've been working him with Dex Thatcher's calves all week. Figured the longer I kept him out of Matt's sight, the happier we'd all be. The horse put in a good day today, then suddenly began favoring the left front leg. Annie examined him, said he should be okay with stall rest and light exercise for the next four weeks."

"And even with that kind of set-back you still think he can win the futurity?"

Alex nodded, unwilling to show even a fraction of his own, gnawing doubt. "He'll be right as rain by the end of the month. You can count on it."

"I hope *you* can count on it, Alex, because Matt

is going to have a holy fit when he finds out the horse is lame on top of being poorly bred.''

It was a challenge to hold his temper, but Alex managed. ''Matt's just going to have to believe me when I tell him I know what I'm doing. I know what this horse can do. We'll be ready by the end of December when the futurity is scheduled.''

''I sure hope you're right, Alex. I don't see how you can be, but I sure hope you're right.''

Nothing like family support, Alex thought. He'd heard from both brothers now and the score was an unsurprising McIntyres—two, Alex—zero.

Jeff walked over and picked his good-looking Stetson off the rack. ''So,'' he said, changing his tone and the subject, ''you've been to Annie's?''

''Yep.''

''And?''

Alex looked up. ''And what? She's pregnant. Did you know?''

Jeff had the grace to look a little embarrassed. ''It's hardly a secret,'' he said defensively. ''Especially considering all the ideas she and Josie are tossing around for this First Baby of Bison City 2000 contest. I figured you either knew about Annie's pregnancy or you didn't.''

''I know now. It would've been nice if someone had seen fit to tell me ahead of time, because finding out in person was something of a shock, but I survived the awkward moments.'' He shrugged. ''Annie says the baby's not mine.''

''She does?''

''Mmm-hmm.''

"Well, then, I guess congratulations aren't in order for you...or are they?"

"Not at the moment, no."

Jeff frowned. "Does that mean you believe her or you don't?"

"It means I'll let you know when I think it's any of your business."

"A bit touchy, there, aren't you, little bro?"

Alex shrugged, unwilling to chance an argument with the only brother he could have a halfway normal conversation with. "I helped her paint the baby's room tonight."

"I can see by your boots that you painted outside the lines again."

Looking down at the obvious stripe and yellow dots, Alex hoped he could get them clean. "Must have stepped in the bucket," he said. "The house needs a lot of work. You'd think Dex would have done something to the place before lettin' her move in, instead of leaving it all for her to do. I know people say it was great of him to give her a roof over her head when she was orphaned and all, but I'm not sure he did her any favors by taking her in."

"Oh, come on, Alex, you've always been too hard on the old man. He just doesn't know how to show his emotions. He cares a lot for Annie. Everybody knows that."

Alex wasn't convinced. "Well, the house is in terrible shape. I'm going to do what I can to fix it up. She needs help, even if I can't get her to admit it."

"Annie's always been an independent little thing. You sure she wants you to be her Mr. Fix-It?"

"I'm not asking permission. Since Koby's out of commission for the next couple of weeks, I've got time on my hands. The way I see it, I may as well put it to good use and do what I can to make the place livable for Annie. Even if the baby isn't mine, I figure I at least owe her that much."

"I somehow doubt she'll see it your way."

Alex met his brother's gaze across the room. "As I said, I'm not asking. I'm just doin'."

Jeff nodded, said nothing for a moment, then, "Matt's in the office. Steer clear of him tonight. But if I were you, I'd get busy finding Willie and makin' amends."

The guilt returned in a landslide. "I don't suppose anyone will believe it was an honest mistake?"

Fitting the Stetson over his dark hair, Jeff put his hand on the doorknob and smiled. "You've always been able to brazen your way through a full-speed stampede, Alex. Don't go gettin' humility on us now." He pushed open the door. "Willie's in her room. Tell her your prize stallion tore a tendon right at supper time and I suspect she'll be in here heatin' up your dinner and fussin' over you before you even get to the groveling part."

Jeff went out, leaving Alex alone with a tepid plate of leftovers and a lump of regret the size of Nevada in his throat. Setting the plate aside, he headed upstairs to change his clothes and stow Loosey before he, like a remorseful kid, went looking for Willie with an apology as worthless as a broken slingshot tucked in his hip pocket.

ANNIE GOT TO the café first, settled into a booth near the front and ordered a cup of coffee. The hubbub in the Chuck Wagon was at its normal, noisy Saturday-morning best, but she still heard the slight snap as Nell's eyebrows went up. "You're not 'sposed to have caffeine," the owner-waitress said. "I'll bring you some milk."

"I don't want milk," Annie stated. "I want coffee."

Nell gave her The Look, making Annie think Genevieve must be going around town, giving lessons. "Just watching out for you," Nell said, unyielding.

"Thanks, but I'm perfectly capable of watching out for myself, and one cup of coffee isn't going to hurt me or the baby."

"Not while you're in the Chuck Wagon it's not, that's for sure. Now, we've got skim or 2 percent. Take your pick. Oh, and buttermilk, too, if you'd rather have that."

In her nightmares, maybe. "I'll have decaf," she said, conceding the much-desired caffeine.

"Nope, I don't think so. There's somethin' about those decaffeinated beverages I don't trust. You can have milk."

Annie sighed, wishing she'd thought to meet Josie out of town somewhere, where no one knew her well enough to boss her around. "Bring me a glass of chocolate milk."

Nell went deaf. "I could get you a cup of herbal tea. No harm in you drinking that, I 'spose."

"Oh, I don't know," Annie said with sincere frustration. "You might want to call Dr. Elizabeth and get a permission slip first."

With another sharp lift of her eyebrows, Nell tucked her pencil and pad into her apron pocket. "I'll come back to get your order when you're in a better humor."

Annie came very close to being surly and stating that a cup of coffee would improve her humor considerably, but she was afraid that would ultimately prevent her from being allowed to order breakfast. By the time Josie arrived, squeezed in on the other side of the booth, and picked up the menu, Annie was halfway through a cup of Bright Eyes herbal tea, waiting for the invigorating, upswing effect on her mood which Nell had predicted would come after the first sip. "Order herbal tea," she told Josie. "It'll save time."

"It's Saturday," Josie said, perusing the breakfast specials, which changed only often enough to make customers check the menu just in case. "I have all morning."

"Then order herbal tea. It'll save your sanity."

Josie grinned and closed the menu. "Is that what you're drinking?"

Annie lifted her cup. "It beats buttermilk."

"What wouldn't?" Josie agreed, eyeing the tea bag, pruned up and drying on Annie's saucer. "On the other hand, my appetite these days seems insatiable. I used to be such a picky eater, but now... I swear someone could suggest I mix olives and tuna salad in with my buttermilk and I'd think it sounded right tasty. Either this baby is hollow, or I'm going to have some serious diet issues when the pregnancy is over.''

Annie laughed, mostly because she just plain liked Josie McIntyre Moore. ''As long as you don't order coffee this morning, I think you're safe. Have you had any more brainstorms about how we can make money with the First Baby in 2000 contest?''

''Not yet. Believe it or not, this has been a busy week. Bison City is practically bursting at the seams with news.''

''News?'' Annie repeated, thinking that *news* and *Bison City* normally didn't get combined in the same sentence. ''You're just trying to convince me to buy a copy of Monday's *Bugle,* aren't you?''

''Nope, but you're going to want to, anyway. For starters, there was a fire in the trash bin behind the Stop'n Shop Wednesday morning early. Asa Mills suspected it was arson, but it turned out to be one of his own stinky cigar butts that set the trash to smoldering. Then on Thursday, the first-grade class at Merriman Elementary put on a kiddie rodeo, where they roped chairs, rode stick horses and sang songs. There was even a foot-stompin' square dance.'' She patted her tummy. ''I hope the school is still doing the rodeos when this little fella—or filly—is old enough to participate. It was just about the funniest thing I've ever seen.''

Nell sashayed up to their table. "Mornin', Mrs. Mayor," she greeted Josie. "What can I get for you?"

"Herbal tea would be nice."

Nell wrote on her pad. "Good choice," she said, crossing the *t* with a flourish. "Some expectant mothers fight me tooth and nail to get caffeine. Glad you're not one of 'em." She spun on her rubber-soled heels and yelled at Holden Smith, the short-order cook, to light a fire under the teakettle and not singe his eyebrows while he did it.

"It figures," Annie said with a wry smile. "I get a lecture and you get the gold star for good behavior. On the record, I only *asked* for coffee. I didn't really try to wrestle her for it."

"It's a darn good thing you warned me. Otherwise, I'd have ordered coffee and gotten the lecture, too. But listen, I have news. Real news."

"You mean something besides a fire and the first-grade rodeo?"

"You betcha." Josie glanced behind her, slid a cautious look all around, then leaned across the table. "Guess who eloped last night?"

"Your brother."

Josie frowned as if that had come out of left field. "Which one? Oh, never mind. It doesn't matter. I couldn't be that lucky. Who in this town would want one of them? Guess again."

For a heartbeat, Annie felt a stupid relief. Not that she even knew why she thought Alex might have been the one, or who he might have eloped with if he had been. There was no rhyme nor rea-

son for it. Not even a breath of logic in the way
he was always the first answer she gave to any
question. "Elope...elope..." She considered other
possibilities for a second guess, then threw out a
wistful, "Genevieve?"

Josie's laughter squashed that hope in the bud-
ding. "Good one, Annie. You're quick. Wrong,
but quick. Come on. Who is the very last person
in Bison City you think of when I say the word
elope?"

Annie ran an imaginary finger down a mental
list of residents. "Reverend Whitehead?"

"Bingo."

"You're kidding." She could see, though, that
Josie wasn't. She had to wait until after Nell
brought Josie's tea before asking, "But who...?"

"Sally Jo Turner, that's who."

Annie blinked. "But she's younger than we are
and he's got to be...?"

"Forty-eight last August." Josie sat back, delighted with her scoop. "Can you believe it? Roper
Simpson called Justin about nine-thirty last night—
we'd just got home from having dinner out at the
ranch—and said he saw a light on over at the
church and it seemed just a tad suspicious to him.
Well, Justin immediately called Sheriff Hitchcock
who called the deputy on duty, who turned out to
be Sally Jo's uncle Clem, who pulled his gun as
he gumshoed up behind them when they were getting into the reverend's Audi, and scared himself—
as well as the two of them—plum silly. It's a wonder he didn't shoot himself in the foot. By the time

Justin arrived, there was already a gathering of the Turner clan, who're none too happy about Sally Jo hooking up with a man of the cloth, much less a Methodist. However, there wasn't a thing they could do about it because the deed was done. The reverend and Sally Jo were married in Las Vegas earlier in the day and were just stopping by the church to pray before heading to the parsonage.''

''At least he knew enough to pray that her family wouldn't murder him.''

''It's probably all that saved him,'' Josie agreed.

Annie shook her head in wonder. ''Sally Jo Turner and Reverend Whitehead. Wow. I never would have suspected the reverend of lusting after Sally Jo, and I sure wouldn't have picked him for her.''

''That's love for you. Doesn't always make sense. It's just there, whether anyone thinks it ought to be or not.''

Wasn't that the truth. ''But what could they possibly have in common?''

Josie grinned. ''Maybe it's their shared passion for Saturday-night bingo at the VFW. I heard from a very reliable source that they've been holding hands under the table during the jackpot round.''

''Holding hands must not be all they've been doing, if they up and eloped without anyone suspecting what they were plan...'' Annie's comment faded away when Alex walked in and set the welcome bell over the door to tingling. He looked around the café—searching, she somehow knew, for her—and set her pulse to tingling with the same kind of energy. A welcoming smile curved her lips before she knew it was there, and across the table Josie turned to see who was on the receiving end. "Look out," Josie said when he was still two tables away. "My brother's tracked us down."

"Maybe he was just tracking breakfast," Annie suggested, although she knew Alex was, more than likely, here on one mission or another.

"Morning, ladies." He reached their booth and unceremoniously scooted in beside his sister, nudging her relentlessly toward the corner. "You don't mind if I join you, do you?"

"Obviously a rhetorical question." Josie acted like a sibling and dug her elbow into his arm to keep him from taking over all of her space. "It's just like you, Alex, to skip out on a dinner where you were supposed to be the guest of honor and horn in on a breakfast where you weren't invited."

This time it was Annie's eyebrows that climbed in surprise, not because Alex would miss a dinner or invite himself to join them for breakfast, but rather because Josie seemed upset with him for it.

With an unconcern that Annie knew in her heart was merely his tough-guy disguise, Alex reached in front of Josie, placing his hat on the shelf that ran the length of one wall and was dotted, booth by booth, with customers' cowboy hats and an occasional lady's handbag. "I didn't remember Willie's dinner until I walked in last night and found the plate of leftovers she put in the stove to warm for me. And before you start giving me what-for, I've already thoroughly expressed my regret to

Willie and Matt, so hobble your scold and save it for some long trail ride when neither one of us has anything better to talk about.''

"I hope Willie pinned your ears back."

"What she didn't say, Matt did, at length. There's no way you can make me feel any worse than I already do, so let's talk about somethin' else, shall we?" He smiled at Annie across the table. "Mornin', Annie. I've just been out to check on Koby. Thanks for feeding him. You didn't have to do that."

"It comes with the whole room-and-board package. Besides, I wanted to see if the swelling was down and make sure he weathered the night all right."

"He seemed to be as tickled as a heifer with a new fence post." He reached over and tugged on a strand of Josie's dark hair. "Just like you, whenever I pull your pigtails."

"In that case, you should shoot him now and put him out of his misery." Josie thumped him on the arm in retaliation for the hair tug. "What's wrong with your horse?"

"Bowed tendon," he said in a tone Annie recognized as his I-don't-want-to-talk-about-it voice. He smiled across the table at her. "I don't see any paint speckles in your hair, so I guess you managed to get cleaned up without me."

"I've been washing my hair without any help since I was five years old," she said, wishing he didn't always have such an instantaneous, invigorating effect on her. Forget caffeine. Forget Bright

Eyes herbal tea. All she needed to jump-start her heart was Alex in the morning. "It took some scrubbing, but I got rid of the speckles, no thanks to you."

"Hey, I offered to stay and get you cleaned up." He waved hello to Nell, who hot-footed it over with a mug and a pitcher of ice water in one hand, dual coffeepots in the other—one containing fresh-brewed coffee and the other just plain hot water.

"'Lo, Alex," she said with a smile as broad as sunrise. Expertly switching all the beverage paraphernalia, she put the mug in front of him and filled it to the brim with heavenly scented, steaming-hot coffee. "I've been saving back a piece of cherry pie every day this week, thinking you'd be in, askin' for it. Where you been keepin' yourself?"

"I'm a workin' man, Nell. You know nothin' short of trainin' a good horse could keep me out of the Chuck Wagon for very long. Got any pie today?"

She nudged him with her elbow. "Pie's not a fit breakfast for a workin' man. You know that. I'll just get Holden to fry up a plate of food that'll do some serious stickin' to your ribs."

"That's what I came in here for," he said with a grin.

"Be back in two wags of a hound dog's tail, with a breakfast you won't soon forget."

He gave her a wink. "My mouth's already watering."

"Josie and I'd like to order," Annie began only to be stopped by Nell's frown.

"I'll bring you expectant mamas a bowl of oatmeal," Nell said, as if their order should have been obvious. "You need some good, old-fashioned grain in your diet. After all, we want these young'uns to come out healthy as little ponies, now don't we?" She gauged the amount of tea left in Josie's mug in a glance and hoisted the hot water pot. "You need a refill on that tea?"

"No thanks." Josie slid her hand over the top of her cup. "I'm fine."

"Me, too." Annie picked up her mug to fend off another refill, which would take her drink to the level of hot water with a tint of tea. "And oatmeal sounds—" Nell's eyebrows went up, transforming the words on Annie's tongue into a resigned "—right tasty."

Nell nodded approval and was off for the kitchen like a round of buckshot, calling hellos to regular customers, directing the other two waitresses with a jerk of her head, refilling coffee cups and water glasses, chatting here and there on her way to the kitchen, and yelling from time to time at Holden, who seldom paid any attention to what she said. Alex clasped his hands on the table and looked from Annie to Josie and back again. "How much will you two give me to slip you some bacon and eggs under the table?"

"Not as much as if you give me a taste of that coffee." Annie inhaled the aroma and promised herself an entire pot of the brew after the baby came. Two pots. Every day. If, that is, she decided not to breast-feed. "Just scoot your cup over this way, so I can reach it."

"Forget it," he said, cradling his palm around the mug. "I'm not contributing to your delinquency."

"You're afraid Nell will kick you out of here without breakfast if you do." Josie fished the tea bag from her cup. "I don't know where Nell gets her information, but even Dr. Elizabeth isn't such a fanatic about what I eat."

"I think you should listen to Nell," Alex observed. "She knows a thing or two about food. And a little self-restraint, just to be on the safe side, isn't a whole lot to ask, you know."

Josie scowled at him. "You give up coffee and then talk to us about how a little self-restraint is good for the soul."

"Baby," he corrected. "Good for the baby."

"Ever notice how it's the fathers who suddenly know so much about sacrifice when it comes to being pregnant?" Josie asked.

Perhaps the remark would have passed unnoticed if Annie could have kept her gaze from jerking to Alex. Or if his gaze hadn't already been on hers, waiting for her reaction. Or if the knowledge of fatherhood hadn't been so intensely deep and sure in his blue eyes. As it was, all she could do was go for yet another denial. "Men always like to believe they understand things they know absolutely nothing about."

Alex held her gaze while she grew tense with

wanting to blurt out the truth, and Josie looked
from one to the other with frank curiosity. "Did I
say something funny?" she asked. "Because you
both have the oddest expressions on your faces."

"You said 'fathers,'" Alex explained, not looking away from Annie for a second. "As if you
were including me in the lineup."

Josie's startled glance switched from Alex to
Annie. "Slip of the tongue," she said, obviously
embarrassed and just as obviously interested in the
outcome. "It's only because all the men in my life
are suddenly sure they know what's best for me
and the baby."

"Must be very annoying." Annie managed to
disengage from Alex's pointed and pressing gaze,
even if she couldn't outrun the thudding awareness
of her heartbeat.

"I don't know why you're complaining." Alex
raised his coffee to his lips, speaking to Josie, but
giving Annie a small, knowing salute with the cup
as he did so. "The men in your life have always
been sure they know what's best for you, Jo. Now
they're just sure they know what's best for the
baby, too."

"Like I don't?" She sniffed in disgust. "It'd be
nice, just once, to be given credit for having some
sense of responsibility myself."

Alex shrugged. "It's not like you listen to us,
anyway. Pregnancy is downright mystifying to a
man. Maybe by offering suggestions, we're just—
in our own clumsy way—trying to have some little
part in it."

"Suggestions?" Josie was winding up to argue the topic at length, it appeared.

Where was Nell and her pot of hot water when you needed it, Annie wondered, searching her brain for an unobtrusive segue into another subject. Any subject at all.

"I'm sure," Josie continued, the gleam of principle in her eyes, "that Annie will agree with me when I say we can spot condescension in a man at twelve paces."

"So, shoot me for being concerned." Alex shrugged off the impending argument and, without so much as a nod to finesse, changed the subject. "What were you two talking about so secretively when I came in? Looked like gossip to me."

"You think I'm going to let you in on any secrets?" Josie challenged.

"Ah, come on, Jo. You know you're dying to tell me the news. Whatever it is."

Annie watched Alex expend a little effort, and charm his sister right back into good humor. Pregnancy was a funny thing, she thought. Hormones all out of whack. Mood swings cycling from high to low and back again without warning. Crying one minute over nothing at all. Or feeling elated because a man walked into the room and sat down across the table. Well, not just a man. Alex. Who shouldn't always take forgiveness for granted. Who shouldn't have forgotten to go to last night's dinner, even with the very real, very troubling disaster of Koby's injury. Yet all Annie could think of now was that he must have been even more worried last night than she'd realized. He must have been sick with concern about the training time lost and all that he had riding on the outcome of the December futurity to have forgotten Willie's dinner. Alex was rebellious and he was often too stubborn for his own good. But he wasn't thoughtless, and he'd never willingly hurt Willie's feelings. He just wouldn't.

If only he could get it right—just once—with his family. If only they could see—just once—that he needed them to believe in him, too. If only— just once—she didn't understand him so completely.

Nell had just delivered two bowls of gruel—or oatmeal, as she called it—and a platter of food big enough to feed Amarillo, when the noise started. Filtering in past the cheer and chatter inside the café, came the plaintive, pathetic and prolonged howling of a dog. Alex salted his eggs and began cutting into them with his fork, oblivious—or pretending to be—to the long, ongoing complaint.

Annie wasn't fooled for an instant. "Did you leave Loosey in the truck?"

"I couldn't very well bring her in here, now, could I?"

"You could have left her at the ranch."

He frowned. "Um…no. Turns out she's not exactly Willie's idea of a houseguest."

"You took a dog into the house with you last night?" Josie asked, clearly stunned by his daring. "After skipping dinner?"

Alex looked at her. "I didn't skip dinner. I honestly, regrettably, forgot. But that's not the reason Footloose is homeless this morning. I nearly had Willie talked into letting her stay on a trial basis when she started this.'' He paused, tipping his head toward the continuing lament. ''Silly dog won't let me out of her sight for longer than ten minutes at a stretch before she sets in to baying like a lovesick coyote.''

Good, Annie thought. ''She's obviously formed a bond with you,'' she said. ''After the trauma she's experienced, I think that's only normal.''

''Howling like a wolf under a full moon is not normal. She needs a good home. Somewhere she'll be treated like one of the family. Somewhere she can be with people. Somewhere she can sniff out news...'' He turned his calculated plea toward Josie, who was ready for him.

''No. No. And no. Justin and I don't want a dog. Not with the baby arriving so soon. Maybe later, but not now. Definitely not now.''

Alex pursed his lips, and Annie knew his ultimate goal—probably the only reason he'd tracked her to the Chuck Wagon this morning—even before he turned his guileless gaze on her. ''Any suggestions, Annie?''

He was sly. So sly.

And she was a sitting duck when it came to him.

''Just one,'' she said, knowing full well the dog had been coming her way from the minute Alex set eyes on it. ''Hand over that bacon, half of those eggs and a biscuit with gravy. Then we'll talk.''

Chapter Seven

"Look, I've got to go and I can't take you with me, so quit asking." Alex swept the hat off his head and rested it on his bent knee. "I know you're disappointed, but I expect you to buck up and act like a lady about it." Squatting on his heels in front of the collie-shepherd, he scratched Loosey's chin until she quivered all over with ecstasy. "That means no howling, understand?"

She wagged her tail, signifying she understood the sweet touch of his hands, if nothing else. Watching from the porch steps, Annie wished she hadn't been so quick to jump in and take responsibility for Loosey, hoped the dog would accept her as substitute and not spend the night howling after Alex and, for no good reason, dreaded the moment he would leave.

It wasn't even as if he were going away somewhere. Just back to the ranch to do some busy-work chores that Matt had assigned as if Alex were still a rebellious teenager needing to do penance for his crime of forgetting dinner. Annie saw it as punishment, pure and simple, but Alex seemed to believe that atonement would, at least, keep the peace if not restore him to the family's good graces. She didn't figure he'd ever stop caring what Matt thought. Or Jeff. Or Josie. Or Ken, Debra and Willie... All of them made up the family he wanted so much to please. All of them made up the family he fought so hard to be separate from.

Not having had anyone in the way of family other than Uncle Dex—at least no one she remembered with much clarity—Annie didn't exactly comprehend the dynamics of parental approval and sibling rivalry, but she knew they'd shaped Alex as surely as ancient wind and water had shaped the Bighorn Mountains.

"Go, Alex." Annie walked down the steps to where canine and cowboy were saying their lingering goodbyes. Reaching down, she took hold of the dog's spiffy new collar. "Just go. It's not like she's never going to see you again. She'll be fine once you're out of sight."

Alex looked up at her for a long moment, then got to his feet and dusted his hat against his thigh. "This is temporary, Annie. More like doggie day care than a transfer of ownership. I know you prefer to believe I'm just dumping Loosey on your doorstep, but right now isn't the best time for her to be at the ranch. Willie would have let her stay, I think, but Matt was adamant."

"So you've told me."

"Okay. Be that way. I'm not going to pretend I'm crazy about having a pet, but I won't shatter

under the responsibility, either. I'll be back tonight
to feed Koby and take Loosey out for a walk. Well,
more of a three-legged hobble, I guess.'' He smiled
and Annie's will of iron bent like cheap cutlery.
"You can go, too, if you think you can keep up.''

"Don't tell me Nell gave you instructions to
make sure I got some exercise, too?''

"Nope. I thought of it all on my own. Which
isn't to say I think you look unhealthy.''

"I look like Uncle Dex's Jersey cow a week
before she's due to calf.'' Annie rubbed her hand
across the spot where the baby kept up steady and
uncomfortable kicking.

Alex's gaze followed her movement. "Is he
moving around?''

His tone sounded hesitant, hopeful. She got no
pleasure out of lying to him, but she was all out
of resistance. One touch of his hand and, like
Loosey, she'd be wiggling all over with pleasure.
"No,'' she said, letting her hand fall back to her
side. "Just a muscle spasm. Happens once in a
while.''

He looked disappointed and she all but admitted
her lie and invited him over to put his hand on her
stomach and experience the baby's kick for himself, which was not a good idea, she knew. But
one that was on the tip of her tongue, nonetheless,
right up until he opened his mouth and started in
again making suggestions.

"Maybe you ought to go in and lie down for a
while,'' he said. "It's Saturday. The clinic's
closed. What else do you have to do?''

Shop for a crib. A layette. Buy groceries…and dog food. Sand the secondhand chest she'd bought for the baby's room. Make curtains. Attend to life's details and about two dozen other odd jobs that were lying in wait for the moment she'd have nothing else to do. "Maybe I will," she said, because otherwise he'd keep pressing his agenda on her and might never leave. Josie was right. Men were always thinking they knew more than you did about the right way to conduct your life or your pregnancy or any other job they deemed you incapable of handling without their help. "Maybe Loosey and I will snooze away the whole afternoon."

"Good idea." He smiled, leaned down to rub the dog's ear one more time, then surprised Annie by straightening, slipping an arm around her and drawing her into a swift, but attention-getting, goodbye kiss. "See you tonight," he said before she could recover her voice. With a quickness the devil himself would envy, Alex settled the hat on his head, got in his old pickup and turned the ignition. As the motor sputtered, coughed and shook itself awake, he laid his left arm across the open window and leaned out. "Take care of my girl," he said, but which one of them he was talking to was anybody's guess.

As the old pickup bumped and rattled its way to the main road, Loosey began to whine deep in her throat. Annie stooped down beside her and looped her arm around the collie's neck, in hopes of stopping the howling before it got started. "I know how you feel," she said aloud. "That's why I can say this to you. Get used to it. He's going to leave, and you're going to stay behind. The sooner you accept that, the less time you'll spend crying for the moon. Understand?''

Loosey's tail flopped in a halfhearted wag, but she didn't howl.

HE WAS BACK BEFORE SUNSET, which came earlier every evening, wearing a fresh-pressed shirt and jeans, sporting a jaunty grin and bearing sacks full of groceries. Loosey all but turned cartwheels on the kitchen linoleum, she was so excited. Annie, who'd had the afternoon to sober up her dizzy little heart, was able to greet him with casual interest, all of which she directed toward the possibility that somewhere in those sacks was chocolate.

No such luck.

"Are you kidding?" He replied when she asked. "I told you this morning I wasn't going to contribute to the delinquency of an expectant mother." He stored more canned goods than she could count, all the while she waited for an appropriate moment to tell him he could stop acting like the man of the house anytime now. It was one thing for her to agree to board his horse and dog-sit his collie. Another to decide to have his baby and not consult him on the decision. But she wasn't going to sit back and let him stock her cupboards with green beans and her freezer shelves with Good Choice Chicken and Vegetable Casseroles, while she pretended not to notice that he was playing house and enjoying the honey-I'm-home role immensely.

"When we go in for your next appointment," he said, slipping it into the conversation like an over-confident pitcher's throwaway toss to second base, "I thought I'd ask the doctor about your diet."

"We?" she repeated, knowing that, appropriate or not, the moment had arrived. "You must be wearing your hat way too tight these days, Alex. It's squeezed your brain into a layer of flapjacks."

He tossed a can of peas and carrots in the air and caught it with a showy swipe of his hand. "My hat fits just fine, thanks, and I'm thinking clearer than I have in months."

"Not if you believe I'll let you go with me to see Dr. Elizabeth, you're not." She shook her head for added emphasis. "That's about as likely as me eating a green bean because you think it's healthy."

"It is healthy. You're a doctor. Tell me you don't advise your patients to eat balanced meals and stay away from chocolate."

"That's different."

"Because...?"

"Because my patients don't know any better than to eat what their owners put in front of them," she snapped, causing Loosey to look at her with a concerned doggy frown.

Alex bent to reassure the collie with a pat on the head. With an ecstatic sigh, Loosey collapsed at his feet like a rag rug. "Annie," he said, "the baby doesn't get any choice in what you eat, either."

Okay, so he had her in an official gotcha. She

was out of practice, letting him bulldog the argument this way. "You are not going with me to see the doctor and that's final."

He nodded, turned to what seemed like a bottomless sack, rummaged in the bottom of it, and pulled out a cellophane bag of Hershey's Kisses with Almonds. He probably believed the nuts made it healthier, somehow. "Too bad, because I bought these in case she said it was okay for you to have a treat now and then." He tossed the bag in the air, caught it like a pro. "Guess I'll have to take these with me."

She was not one of Pavlov's dogs, salivating at the sound of a cellophane rattle. She wasn't. "You do that. Because, for your information, I can buy my own Kisses anytime I want a treat. Come to think of it, I can buy all the groceries I need whenever I need them, and I'll thank you to keep your nose out of my cupboards from now on."

"Just trying to help, Annie."

"No, you're not. You're trying to charm your way back into my life for some nefarious reason all your own."

"Nefarious?" He grinned and tossed the bag of candy next to the whole wheat bread already on the counter.

"That means, to put it simply, you are up to no good."

"I know what it means, Annie, and I have just one question for you. Do you know what this means?" He waggled his eyebrows up and down, looking silly and funny, and forcing her to fight back an answering smile.

"No," she said, trying hard for a snippy tone. "What does that mean?"

The grin returned. "It means, if my wicked and nefarious purpose is to charm you, how'm I doin' so far?"

There was too much confidence in the question, too much cocksure optimism glinting in his sinfully blue eyes, but before the full impact could sink into her lollygagging brain, he'd stored yet another can of green vegetables in her cupboard and come up behind her to put his hands on her shoulders. His breath stirred the pulled-back strands of her hair, his warmth stole through her like a thief, and with his touch, every tingling, wide-awake nerve cell in her body sat up and took notice. "Admit it, Annie," he said softly. "You enjoy being taken care of as much as I enjoy doing it."

"As I keep trying to tell you," she said on an uneven sigh, "I can take care of myself."

"I never said you couldn't. I only said I'm here to help."

Be strong. Be smart. Be sensible. The practical litany pulsed through her head, but her heart had skipped school the day they studied wisdom and never quite got the knack of it. Not when it came to Alex. "You're not going to change my mind by blowing in my ear," she said in a voice that might have sounded haughty if it hadn't been so breathless. "Dr. Elizabeth's office is off-limits to you."

His palms felt warm and sheltering against her arms, while the scents of a rugged outdoors, horses and saddle leather conspired with soap, shampoo and aftershave to wrap all around her and draw her back into the familiar circle that was his embrace. "Just trying to be here for you, Annie. Just trying to be your friend."

Liar, liar, pants on fire. He wanted to be more than that...for the moment, at least. Alex was always at his persuasive best when he felt he'd been denied what he thought he wanted. "This baby has a father," she said firmly, doing her best not to dwell on how lovely and warm she felt in his arms but on remembering how cold it would be in the winter when he was long gone. "And he's not you."

Loosey sighed in her sleep, rolled like a lumpy gunnysack onto her side, her neon-colored cast bright against the faded kitchen flooring. Behind Annie, Alex stood like a rock, holding her gently, closely against him, his hands sliding down her arms to clasp her fingers in his. "Then again, Annie," he said, softly—so softly, "I'm here and he's not."

Which was both truth and lie, yes and no. "Alex," she whispered, more to herself than him. "Go home. Spend time with your family. Kick off your boots and pick out some melodies on your old guitar. Go over to Josie's house and count how many cans of green beans she has in her pantry. Do anything except this."

"This?" His lips found a patch of neck that

wasn't covered by her hair or any other kind of insurance and kissed it lingeringly. "Or this?" His fingers laced with hers and he carried her arms around with his as he cradled her into an interlocking embrace. When he breathed in the scent of her hair with obvious delight, his chest moved against her shoulders and she remembered all the times before when she'd gotten lost in the wanting of him. It was lovely to be held, lovely to be touched, lovely to know he still desired her and, except for one thing, she knew she'd have turned into his kiss like a ship turns toward a lighthouse on a dark and moonless night.

But like a silent chaperone, the baby rounded their sensual longing into an awareness that they were no longer a party of two. Three hearts beat in rhythm now. Annie couldn't afford to forget that. She savored Alex's warmth for another moment, then firmly unclasped her hands from his, drew her body from the harbor of his arms and turned to look into the deepest secrets in his blue, blue eyes. "What do you want, Alex? What is it you think I have to give you?"

"A son."

She'd asked for that one. Eyes wide open, she'd set herself up for it. "Mighty big request, even for a guy who thinks every sunset is put in the sky for him to ignore or not, as he chooses. I can't *give* you a son, Alex. It's not that simple."

"Admit he's mine. Admit we made love and a baby on that night last April after Josie's wedding."

"I can't do that. It's not fair for you to keep asking me to."

"Not fair? I've offered to marry you, Annie. I've said I want to be a part of my son's life."

Marry him. She could grab for the brass ring here and now, take his name for herself and her son. Did it matter that he never said he loved her? Did it matter if he couldn't see that offering marriage and wanting to marry her were not one and the same thing? She'd wanted to be Alex's wife for a decade or more. But not so he could be "part" of her son's life. Not so he could pick and choose when he'd be there and when he wouldn't. "Please, Alex. Go, before I do something really stupid and believe you actually mean that."

His hands dropped from her and he stepped back. The grin was long gone. So was the light of confidence and faith in his eyes. "You're right, Annie. Believing anything I say would be a really dumb idea." He picked up his hat and set it on his head with movements as tightfisted as a soldier's salute. "Just think what a fix you'd be in if it turned out you were wrong." Then, with an angry set to his jaw and his shoulders, he walked out the door.

Funny thing, though. Loosey didn't even know he was leaving until the door banged shut behind him. But by then, it was too late to start howling.

ALEX STAYED AWAY the next day. He checked on Koby early, before there was a light on in the little house next to the stables, and spent the day mending McIntyre fences. Not the ones that bound the ranch into acres of pastures and grazing range, but the familial fences of family ties and wounded vanities. He persuaded Matt to drive over to Sheridan on the pretext of checking out a brood mare—with blue blood enough to pass for royalty—he was thinking of buying. The trip over was short on conversation and long on cold shoulder, but the road home, paved with the giving and taking of Matt's opinions on the mare, saw them skirting an edgy peace. Jeff, Josie and Justin came for a late lunch, which Alex helped Willie fix, and stayed to play a nostalgic remember-the-time…game of old stories and shared history.

It wasn't until the sun began to set, when the talk turned to Josie and Justin's baby that Alex felt out of sync and out of patience. He grew suddenly restless for home, but damned if he knew where that was. Here? Among the people and tales that made up his history? Or with Annie and the baby they had made together? Or was home the pickup truck parked outside—four wheels and horsepower enough to take him from the mountains to the ocean and back again, or anywhere else the highway led.

And the answer to that question was…none of the above. He didn't belong here at the S-J and Annie didn't want him with her. But the only other alternative—nowhere in particular—had no appeal at all. And that brought him right back to the conclusion he'd been avoiding all day. Right back to the resolve that some way, somehow, he had to

prove himself to Annie. Prove himself worthy to
be a father to her son.

Whether she liked the idea or not.

So, with no explanation other than a casual "See
you later," Alex put on his hat and headed for
town.

THERE WAS ONLY ONE WAY to handle a situation
like this.

So, armed with four quarts of tomato juice and
clenched teeth, Annie half dragged the skunk-stunk
collie to the large-animal area behind the clinic.
Once they were on the concrete floor, under the
metal lean-to type roof, she tied the dog as close
to the faucet and drain as possible. "If you hadn't
been so all-fired eager to prove you could run as
well on three legs as four, we'd be in the house
right now, listening to country-western music on
the radio, warm as two pieces of buttered toast and
smelling like two petals off the same rose."

Loosey looked at her, brown eyes brimming
with humiliation and worry.

"Okay, so maybe neither one of us is any threat
to a rose on our better days, but honestly, Loosey,
don't you know better than to chase a polecat?"

The collie's head dipped even lower, and Annie
felt sorry for her, despite being mad as a rooster
in a rainstorm. It was bad enough she'd wasted
most of the day feeling sorry for herself, wondering if Alex had left town, wishing she had a fence
post to rub the steady ache in her back against,
watching a cold front push the sun toward a chilly

evening. She couldn't even eat the chocolate kisses he'd so thoughtlessly left behind, because she kept thinking what if he were right and the baby was suffering somehow for her sweet tooth? So she'd piddled away the entire day, doing large amounts of nothing and feeling worse by the minute, only to decide late in the afternoon that a little exercise would put everything right. What could be better, she'd conned herself into believing. Get out of the house for a brisk walk in the crisp, October air. Stretch her legs and her restless mood. See something other than the four walls of this house. Loosey would love it, and Annie knew she'd feel better for the effort herself.

Well, she'd been right on one count. Loosey had loved every second of the time outdoors. Every nip of the wind, every crackle of autumn grasses, every wild, sweet second of freedom—right up until the moment she'd decided to shake hands with Pepe Le Pew. Now she had to be washed down in tomato juice and rinsed clean with the hose before Annie bundled her into the clinic for a thorough soap and water bath. That is, they'd get to the bath if they both didn't freeze to death first. The wind was whipping around the shelter of the building with increasing gusto, and it was beginning to feel as if she and Loosey might turn into Popsicles. Stinky-winky Popsicles that would require fumigation before they thawed out in the spring. Dumb dog. Dumber Annie for letting Alex double-talk her into keeping the collie for him in the first place.

Loosey whined, deep in her throat. A mourning

sound, forerunner of a pitiful howl, and, stinky or not, Annie couldn't help but lay aside the trickling water hose so she could stoop beside the collie and offer a little comfort. "Hush," she crooned. "I know you didn't mean to get sprayed. I know that old skunk was just mad at the world 'cause he got caught out by the change in the weather. I know you feel just awful. Lesson learned, okay?"

The dog thrust her muzzle into Annie's open palm and looked at her in mute apology, strengthening the bonds of what was already a formidable kinship. Okay, so the bargain hadn't been quite as one-sided as Annie had made sure Alex believed it to be. Truth was, she didn't mind at all that she'd wound up with the dog. Although there was no doubt Alex needed the challenge of responsibility, Annie just flat needed the company. It got lonely in the little house at night, and waking up in the morning, she was first and always acutely aware of her aloneness. The baby would change that, of course, but his birth was still nearly three months away, and ever since Alex had come home, she'd felt as if the walls were closing in on her. So, although it had to be their little secret, she needed Footloose as badly as the dog needed a home.

To be fair, too, she honestly thought she was giving Alex what he didn't know yet that he wanted—a way out. She would take responsibility for his dog and his baby and pretend to believe it was a mutual agreement. He would pretend to believe it was only a temporary arrangement. She would watch him grow restless and discontented under the critical eye of his family. He would watch the sunset with a yearning only she seemed to see. Then, one day, he'd think of someplace he needed to be, some reason he had to leave, and he'd go. And since nothing she could say or do would stop him, she might as well have Loosey to commiserate with once he was gone.

But it would be much easier to commiserate with a clean dog than one that reeked to Pikes Peak. "This is going to be much worse for you than me," she told Loosey. "And that's the way I mean to keep it, understand? Stay still and we'll be done in a jiff."

Unfortunately, the first impediment to the plan turned out to be a little problem of positioning— mainly how to get from a stooping position to a standing one. Annie, increasingly awkward with pregnancy, couldn't shift her center of gravity without using her hands as a lever and a point of contact, Loosey, from which to lever from. But a three-legged dog wasn't much use as a booster rocket, and in trying to put weight on her cast, the collie started to tip over and had to scramble to catch her balance, causing Annie to lose hers. Since there was no point in both of them going down and since it was obvious that one of them was, Annie did the only thing she could and bolstered the collie upright, while she, herself, rolled sideways and landed on her butt.

The impact radiated in an immediate and upward ache across her abdomen and up her spine. A muscle spasm closed in on her tummy and, with a soft gasp, she laid down flat on the cold concrete. She stretched her leg out straight in hope of easing the cramp, but felt resistance against the sole of her boot and jerked back, sending the spasm in another arc across her belly, and a low groan past her lips. "Oh, nooo…"

Too late. The juice slopped over the side of the plastic pitcher as it tipped, coating her foot—boot, sock and exposed ankle—before soaking its way up her denim-covered leg in a gunky river of pulverized tomatoes. Yuck. But until the muscle spasms subsided, she could do nothing except lie there getting cold and wet and worried. So she took a quick inventory of her aches and pains and decided nothing was broken or too badly bruised. Her muscles eased into a normal, general complaint against the extra poundage she carried and the awkward position she was in and she began to count her blessings. Never mind the hard sting of cold concrete under her. Forget about the vegetable goo all around her. The baby was okay. So was she. It could have been worse. Much worse.

Then Loosey came over to check things out in all her musky, aromatic splendor.

"Ugh, Loosey! You smell terrible!"

A comment the dog debated by giving Annie's nose a good lick and then trying to render a bit of canine CPR with breath rank enough to be designated an environmental hazard.

It was the last straw. Not knowing whether to spit or gag, scream or cry, Annie recognized that it wasn't fair to blame Loosey for acting like—of

all things—a dog. The skunk was hardly at fault
for defending itself like a—well, a skunk. And,
although, she'd have liked to blame Alex for pretty
much everything, there really wasn't any reason to
do that, either. He was always going to behave
like—well, like Alex. Popping in and out of her
life on his way to some distant dream of a future,
leaving her behind with memories—and other,
more tangible reminders—of their time together
and the indisputable fact that she loved him, for
reasons she'd probably never fully understand. So,
considering her options, she did the only thing she
could to salvage her sanity. She laughed.

And laughed.

And laughed.

Which made Loosey nervous. Her head went up.
Her ears perked. Her tail began its metronome wag,
swaying from side to side, faster and faster in time
with a distant clackity, clackity, cough rattle.

Wait a minute.

The collie wasn't nervous. She was barely paying any attention to Annie's predicament at all. No.
The silly mutt was watching for Alex, having recognized the peculiar noises his truck made even as
the sounds were still percolating in Annie's con-
sciousness. Alex was coming to the rescue, and
that seemed somehow hilarious to Annie, too.
Nothing like looking and smelling like wet skunk
when the man you loved came to call. She laughed
some more, and her heartbeat kicked into a glad
rhythm, too, not unlike the hopeful, excited, one-
two wag of Loosey's tail. Even the baby seemed

to glean the excitement in the air and began to kick. Or maybe it was the saturating cold that was making him as uncomfortable as his mother.

Given her impending rescue, Annie wondered if it was worth the effort to sit up. Or if she should just let Alex be a hero from the word go, and strain his back trying to get her and her world-class tummy off the floor.

Maybe it was the smell that kept her indecisive. Or the glue of tomato pulp underneath her. Or the pungent collie standing over her, wagging from one end to the other in anticipatory delight. Maybe she was just weak from laughing. Whatever the reason, Annie was still lying there in the wet soup of trickling water and diluted juice, when he drove in.

ALEX NEARLY HAD A HEART attack when he realized the crumpled lump of clothing Loosey appeared to be guarding with her life was, in reality, Annie. He shoved the gearshift into Park, flung open the pickup's cranky door, sprinted across the yard to the metal-roofed bay. His heart did stop when he spotted the blood pooled around her. He wished he could have stopped breathing when Loosey executed a surprisingly agile leap and all but flung herself into his arms.

"Whoa, Loose," he said, pushing her away. "You stink." Then he was bending over Annie, reaching for her wrist to check her pulse, his heart thudding with dread and fear—until she smiled a slightly loopy smile, and relief caved in on him with bone-crushing deliverance.

"Stand back, Superman," she said. "We've been skunked."

"That much I'd already figured out." Her heartbeat was steady and strong, thank God. "Are you all right?"

"Couldn't be better. This is very good concrete, you know. Doesn't give an inch."

She must have hit her head. A concussion, maybe. On closer examination, the spreading stain around her didn't look like blood. It looked and smelled like tomato juice, which logically followed the clues his brain had processed in a few seconds of observation—dog, eau de skunk, overturned pitcher. But why Annie was flat on her back on the cement wasn't as clear. "Are you hurt?" he asked. "Bleeding, maybe?"

"Tomato juice from toe to—" She lifted her head to see how far the juice had spread and made a face. "Shoot. It's seeped all the way up and into my hair." Lying back again, she frowned up at him. "You know, Alex, I may have stumbled into a worthwhile discovery. Getting vegetable intake through skin absorption. What d'ya think?"

"Not much." He ran a critical gaze over her, wondering what else could be wrong. She looked okay. Her color was good, if a little on the rosy side. Still, she could be in shock. Or delirious. Maybe he should call her doctor. The baby might be in trouble. Or in the process of being born. *Holy cow, Sundance. Circle the wagons.* What if she was in labor?

Annie pushed up onto her elbows. "I'm okay," she said, reading him as easily as Julia Childs could read a recipe. "No broken bones. No bleeding. No labor pains. Nothing to worry about. I didn't even fall hard. Just sort of rolled over." A throaty remorse purled past her lips. "Although I'm beginning to think I've jarred loose my olfactory sensors because, honest to Betsy, I think I'm getting used to the smell."

"Your sensors are probably just iced over. Haven't you noticed it's cold out here?" He ran a hand across her forehead on the pretext of lifting the hair away from her eyes but in reality, checking for a fever.

"No temperature, either," she said. "Well, nothing above the ordinary ninety-eight point six."

"It'll be a chilly sub-zero Celsius if you don't get out of this wind."

"I wasn't planning to camp out all night," she declared testily. "But this dog has to be deodorized and I sure as heck wasn't going to put her in my bathtub."

"Why didn't you just do it inside the clinic instead of out here?"

"Can't you smell her? If I'd stepped foot inside those doors without juicing the odor first, Genevieve would have taken one whiff tomorrow morning and quarantined the place for a month."

"Funny, I thought you owned the clinic."

"Yes, well, tell that to Genevieve."

Alex decided it wasn't going to get any warmer talking about that old warhorse. "Let's get you off the floor." He put an arm beneath her shoulders and started to slide one beneath her knees.

"Stop!"

He stopped, scared all over again. "What? Did that hurt? Where? What happened?"

"Nothing, yet. But lifting me is going to be a lot harder than you think it will be. Just give me a hand up, would you?"

"Damn, Annie, you knocked the starch plum out of me. Now, put your arm around my neck and hang on because I'm going to pick you up and carry you into the house," he stated.

"Not today, you're not," she replied, just as firmly. "I don't want to take any chances with getting dropped on my butt on top of busting it. The concrete's wet and goopy and having four feet on the floor will be a whole lot more trustworthy than two up and two down."

She had a point, so he changed positions, secured his footing and extended both hands, marveling as she placed her palms against his that fingers could feel so icy to the touch. Before he could pull her up, though, she gave him a warning look. "A word of caution," she said. "Any remarks comparing this exercise to getting a horse on her feet after she's been down, and I'll give you a solid kick in the shin. Providing, of course, you let me hold on to you while I do it."

"I do have some sense of self-preservation, Annie. Ready?"

She nodded and he pulled her up and onto her feet. Keeping his grip on her hands, he rubbed them hard to stimulate her circulation. "You're frozen. How long have you been out here, anyway?"

"Here? Oh, maybe fifteen, twenty minutes. But Loosey and I set out for a walk probably an hour ago."

"Didn't you notice the cold front moving in this afternoon?"

"Yes, Alex, I noticed."

"But you still decided to go for a walk?"

"That's right." Her voice was suddenly trip-wired with aggravation. "Yesterday, you were telling me I needed exercise. Now I suppose you're going to try and tell me breathing fresh air is bad for the baby?"

"This air isn't fresh, Annie. It's frigid."

"Well, it wasn't this cold when I decided to take your dog for a walk."

Ah, so now it was turning personal, which meant she was feeling more normal. "My dog has a broken leg. Seems to me she could have skipped exercise for one day."

"Well, I couldn't, and since she hates to be left alone, she had to come for the walk with me. Any other questions?"

"How did she happen to scare up a skunk in the first place?"

Annie's chin came up. "I don't know, Alex. Maybe because she's a dog and that's what dogs do. Or maybe I didn't have anything better to do and decided to see what would happen if I introduced the two of them.''

This was not exactly the direction in which he'd hoped to move, Alex thought, wondering how he was going to persuade her to stop fussing at him, go inside the house and get warm. ''If it's all the same to you, I'd just as soon go inside to argue as stand out here and do it.''

''I'd just as soon you went away and left me to do what needs to be done.''

''You're not doing anything that can't happen inside out of this wind.''

Her chin came up another haughty notch. ''I'm not going in until I've taken care of this poor, stinky animal, who is probably colder than either one of us and definitely smells worse.''

''I'll take care of her, Annie. She is, as you've pointed out, my responsibility.''

''Not today she isn't. Just go, Alex, before you need a bath as badly as she and I do. Come back and visit tomorrow if you want, but we're not in the mood for company tonight.''

''Forget it, Annie. I'm not going anywhere, so make your peace with the idea and tell me what I need to do to make you happy.''

Then, without so much as a blink of warning, tears welled like raindrops in her eyes and spilled over to run down her rosy cheeks. Lord help him, she was crying. He didn't know why, couldn't think of a single reason for it. Annie never cried that he could remember. Okay, so the odor was bad, but not that bad. The air was cold and the job ahead unpleasant, but that sure didn't make him feel like bawlin'. He didn't know if he should just pick her up over her protests and carry her into the house, or if he should give her his shirttail so she could wipe her face. He flat didn't know what to do, but he sure wished she'd stop.

He knew from Josie's complaints that pregnancy threw a woman's hormones completely out of whack. He knew his sister wasn't her usual easy-going self lately. But somehow he hadn't thought Annie was similarly affected. And yet, there she stood, crying. Clearly he was in over his head, and the only action that occurred to him was to draw her into his arms—right where they were, despite the cold bite of the wind and all his yammering about it, despite the pungent, permeating odor of skunk—and let her cry it out on his shoulder.

Or kiss her, which would give her something else to think about.

Or bundle her off to the doctor, which would make her really mad but seemed to him the safest option. Although it surely wasn't his favorite.

Chapter Eight

"A little bruising," Dr. Elizabeth Lee explained. "But otherwise, she checks out fine."

"The baby's okay?" Alex asked insistently, embarrassing Annie all over again. As if this ridiculous trip to the local hospital wasn't bad enough, as if calling Dr. Lee on a Sunday evening and telling her God-only-knows-what to get her to come in after hours and do an exam wasn't completely humiliating, he had to act as proprietary as a husband and soon-to-be father. There was nothing for it, Annie decided. She would have to murder him. Slowly. Painfully. And with no remorse.

"Mother and baby are just fine," Dr. Lee assured Alex, again. "There's nothing at all for you to be concerned about."

Alex nodded, but looked concerned anyway. "No special instructions for tonight? Medications? Extra rest? Special diet? Anything like that?"

"No, although—" Dr. Elizabeth turned a lively smile on Annie "—I would recommend a bath."

Annie wanted to dig a hole in the floor and hibernate until this whole embarrassing incident was forgotten—probably a century or two. The least Alex could have done was hose her off before bringing her in to see the doctor. But no, he'd said. There wasn't time, he'd said. She needed to get checked out. She needed to know for certain that the baby was okay. She needed the reassurance only a doctor could provide that her fall on the concrete and subsequent exposure to the cold wouldn't come back to haunt her—and the baby.

No amount of explaining that she hadn't fallen off a four-story building or even off a curb for that matter, made a dent in his chosen scenario. No amount of adamant refusal fazed his determination. She was seeing the doctor, he said, and that was that. He'd even had the gall to tell her she didn't smell that bad. While she hadn't personally tangled with the skunk and didn't smell as bad as Loosey, Annie knew her goodhearted obstetrician had probably wished for a clothespin to clamp on her nose during the exam.

Oh, yes, she was going to get him for this. Annie renewed her commitment to revenge and shot him a meaningful scowl. "Do you hear that, Alex? There's nothing wrong with me that a nice warm bath wouldn't have cured an hour ago. Just like I tried to tell you, you jughead." She turned toward her obstetrician and new friend with yet another apology. "I'm so sorry about this," she apologized sincerely. "I wouldn't have bothered you if I hadn't been bullied into it."

"Please, Annie," Elizabeth said with a laugh.

"Don't apologize anymore. It's my job as your doctor to do everything I can to help you deliver a healthy baby with no complications. I'd much rather spend a half hour now making sure that some little ache you think is nothing doesn't turn out to be something for both of us to worry about later on. I know you'll hate this, but this time I have to agree with Alex. He was right to be concerned and to insist you come in and get checked out."

Alex beamed under the approval as he held up Annie's coat so she could slip her arms in the sleeves. He was playing his role as caretaker so well, Annie was half-afraid he meant to turn her around and button the coat for her. "I can't tell you how glad I am you said that, Doctor." Alex settled the coat on Annie's shoulders and kept his arm there, too. "Because otherwise I'd have caught heck when we got home."

Elizabeth's pretty eyes reflected a wry amusement. "It's my professional opinion, Alex, that you're going to catch *hell* when you get this young woman home."

He laughed and gave Annie's shoulders a squeeze. "Nothing new for me. I've been catching that for one reason or another as long as I can remember."

"And learning nothing from the process." Annie shrugged away his protective arm, more miffed by the way he'd wheedled himself into Dr. Elizabeth's good graces than by his actions in general. She glanced at Alex. "Just so we're all clear on protocol, this unscheduled doctor's visit is going on your bill.''

He reached over and straightened her collar. ''I wouldn't have it any other way,'' he said. ''Send the bill to me in care of the S-J Ranch and I'll happily take care of it. In fact, from now on, send all of Annie's statements to me. I think it's the least I can do considering all the trauma I've caused her—and you—this evening.''

Annie wanted to refute his offer here and now, but arguing in front of her obstetrician would undoubtedly turn out to be bad for the baby. So she just smiled and vowed to clear up the matter with Dr. Elizabeth later. After she'd stuffed Alex so full of green beans he died of vegetable poisoning. It wouldn't be a pretty crime, or a perfect murder and her son would probably be born in prison, but the idea was growing on her just the same. She turned to Elizabeth. ''I suppose it's too late to tell you I've never seen this man before and to ask you to call Sheriff Hitchcock and report a dangerous stalker?''

''He obviously has your best interests at heart,'' the doctor replied with a smile.

''He's a fraud and a bully,'' Annie replied. ''Don't let him fool you.''

''I rarely let anyone do that.'' Elizabeth put her hand in the pocket of her lab coat, which would no longer button over the rounded form of her own pregnancy. Annie didn't know anything much about Dr. Lee's life before she came to Bison City. She did know she was single, pregnant and had a lovely smile and that the two of them were going to be friends long after their babies arrived. And that, Annie figured, was more than enough to know about someone, anyway. "How's the First Baby of Bison City contest coming along?" Dr. Elizabeth asked. "Last time Josie was in, she was trying to come up with some ideas that might turn the contest into a moneymaker."

"We're working on it." Annie pulled a glove from each pocket and proceeded to put one on each hand, before Alex did it for her. "And we'll keep you informed so you can pass the information and entry forms on to any new potential New Year deliveries."

Elizabeth's eyes widened in alarm. "If there are any more babies due in Bison City around the end of the year, I don't even want to know about them. As it is, I'm considering asking some of the doctors in the area to be on call in case Dr. Dave and I need help with the deliveries."

"You don't think everybody will go into labor at the same time, do you?" Alex asked, obviously happy to have found something new to fret about. "I mean, what are the odds of that happening?"

Annie and Elizabeth shared a look of amusement at all the mysterious things a man couldn't possibly understand. "Ask any doctor or nurse what happens during the changing of the moon before you make book on how many babies could possibly be born at the same time." Elizabeth walked with them to the door and prepared to lock up. "The truth is, nobody knows when a baby is going to decide it's the right time to be born. So I'm going on the assumption that they could all be eager to make an appearance at the dawn of the new millennium. Who knows? Stranger things have happened."

"Wow," Alex said, apparently struck by the possibilities. "Thanks again, Doctor. I'll see you next…?" He looked to Annie, obviously expecting her to fill in the date of her next appointment.

"Around town," she said, feeling like she'd struck a blow for independence. "And I'll see you soon."

Then she went out the door, head up, tummy leading the way, her thoughts already jumping ahead to a nice, long, fragrantly bubbled bath and a pizza. Two slices of sausage and cheese. Or pepperoni. No, one of each. Definitely.

"GO AWAY," she said in answer to the knock on the bathroom door. "I'm not speaking to you."

"Well, okay, but that's going to make it difficult to communicate."

"Oh, I don't think so." Annie slid lower in the tub, laid her head against the curved porcelain and closed her eyes. "You can call me long-distance and I'll hang up on you. How about that for starters?"

"For starters, it's a local call," came his muffled but cheery reply.

"In that case, I won't answer the phone."

"Makes no never-mind to me. I can eat this whole pizza myself."

Pizza? She opened her eyes, then closed them again, deciding it was another of his dirty, rotten tricks. Either that, or he'd found some way to ruin a perfectly good meal by smothering it with vegetables. "Go home, Alex," she said. "And take whatever you cooked with you."

"Nope. Don't think that's going to happen."

She shouldn't ask, didn't really care, but she was feeling relaxed, mellow and empowered. What's the worst he could do? Call Dr. Elizabeth and complain that she wouldn't eat her supper? "What do you think is going to happen, Alex?"

"I think you're going to ask me to come in there and massage your feet."

Smiling, she wondered if her attraction to Alex was based primarily on the fact that he was such a dreamer. "Nope," she said, practical to the core. "Don't think that's going to happen."

"You sure?"

"So positive it isn't even funny."

"I can bring the pizza in," he suggested.

"Don't bother, I like it cold." There, she thought. That ought to make him crazy.

Quiet followed. Several blissful moments of it. She might even have nodded off for a second or two, because the next thing she heard was the soft creak of floorboards settling and then a splash as her feet were rudely pulled up from the depths to the edge of the tub. Bubbles—sandalwood-scented variety—went up her nose and her eyes flew open to see Alex perched on the rim, holding her toes, preparing to give them a rubbing. "What...?" she sputtered. "Just what do you think you're doing?"

"Doctor's orders," he said with a wicked wink. "She recommended a bath, and I'm here to help."

"I'm certainly capable of taking a bath by myself, Alex. And that's the way I intend to keep it."

"You keep saying that, you know. About being capable."

"Because it's true."

"Well, if it were true about bathing, you'd have been out of this tub thirty minutes ago. Your supper's getting cold, and I figured since I hadn't heard so much as a quack out of you, you must need a little help."

"I need help installing a lock on that door, that's for certain. Now get out of my bathroom before I send you sprawling with my—" She scoured beneath the surface of the bubbles for a weapon and pulled up a back scratcher. But there were places on her body she could no longer reach and she needed that scratcher. Dropping it back into the water, her hand dived again and came up with the loofah sponge which, while not exactly a luxury item at the bath and beauty shop, was still something of a treasure for her. She dropped it, too, and went in search of something else.

"Keep looking. You'll come up with that rubber ducky, yet."

"You bet I will." But his thumbs were pressing soothing circles against the balls of her feet, and his fingers were working away the tension in her soles. And her soul cautioned her not to be too hasty. Sure, he shouldn't be in the room. By rights, she should have locked him out of the house before getting in the tub. But he'd told her to go ahead, take her bath, while he gave Loosey her belated after-skunk scrub. She hadn't forgiven him for hauling her into the hospital and disturbing Dr. Elizabeth. No, indeed.

On the other hand, it felt so lovely, so altogether decadent to lounge in the tub while someone else did the dirty work. And now…well, he was very talented with his hands. Before she knew it, her head was resting on the back of the tub again and her eyelids were drifting closed. "Mmm," said Annie, the pushover of the century. "That feels…good."

"Does it?" His voice was almost as soothing as his massage. "Want me to keep rubbing?"

"Mmm."

"Which translates into roughly 'yes, don't stop' or 'no, keep going?'"

"I know what you're doing." She sighed, replete with relaxation. "So don't think you're pulling the wool over my eyes."

"That'd be some soggy wool."

"You're trying to make up to me for dragging me in to see the doctor."

"That's what I'm doing, all right."

He didn't sound sorry, but she didn't mind so much anymore. "Just so you know you're not fooling me."

"You always were two steps ahead of me,

Annie. 'Course, I guess that doesn't take a rocket scientist, does it?''

''No. It takes somebody a whole lot smarter than that.'' She sensed his smile, even with her eyes shut. ''It takes somebody who knows all your little tricks.''

His hands slid around her heels and began to work her ankles. Trickster. If he thought he was getting any farther than that, he had a surprise coming. She could still reach that back scratcher and she'd sacrifice it, if she had to. ''Your feet are swollen,'' he said. ''Is that because of the baby?''

''Mmm-hmm. Either that or because I weigh a couple of tons.''

''No, you don't. You've stayed in great shape, Annie. I'm proud of you.''

Her eyelids went up with that remark. ''My shape is great, but only if you're comparing me to the great gray whale. I'm convinced I'll never see size eight again.''

He laughed softly. ''I can remember when you thought you'd never get to wear ladies' sizes at all.''

That had been when she was still in double-A's and her complaint had little to do with clothes and everything to do with what women wore under them. ''Not the same thing at all. How can you remember that when you can't even remember my birthday?''

''Who says?''

''All the presents I never got. Plus half the time

you'd call to wish me a happy birthday either a day or two ahead or a week later."

"True, but the other half of the time, I was right on the money."

That was the thing about Alex. He liked to hold his cards close to his chest and he loved being unpredictable. "I never could figure out if you did it on purpose."

"What? Forgot your birthday? Why would I do that?"

She regarded him for a moment, so comfortable in his presence that, if she'd had any sense at all, it would have scared her, especially when there was nothing covering her but a bathtub full of bubbles. "You never forgot it completely, Alex, and I sometimes wondered if you missed it by a day here or there just so I wouldn't expect you to get it right and be disappointed if you didn't."

He kept rubbing, his gaze focused on the movement of his hands, his attention on her feet, giving away nothing except a little tender, loving care. "I'm for any theory that makes you happy, Annie."

Okay, so he'd never admit it in a million years, but she believed she was right. "How about the theory that you really have no business being in here when I'm in the tub?"

"I wasn't thinking in terms of business. I just figured you needed someone to rub your feet and ease you out of being cranky."

"I'm cranky because you're not listening to me.

Go, Alex. Get out of here before I throw something at you."

"You tried that already."

"This time I'll find something, and you know I have really good aim."

"For a girl." His smile was funny and gentle and she loved the way it crinkled up around his eyes.

"You're just scared, that's all."

"Either that or just plain stupid." He looked over the ocean of bubbles. "You sure you don't need help getting out of the tub?"

"I've been doing it by myself for years." She pulled her feet from his now-slippery hands and buried them below the bubbles. "Go."

"If you're sure…" He meandered lazily to the doorway, stopped to lean against the frame. "Because I can keep my eyes shut, if being naked bothers you."

Being pregnant and naked bothered her, but she certainly wasn't going to say so. "I'm not falling for that old line. Now go."

He grinned, nodded. "I'll be right outside in the hall if you need me." He stepped out, then leisurely stepped back in. "Oh, I've been meaning to ask you, Annie. You made up that Peace Corps fella, didn't you?"

Uh-oh. She strove for a puzzled expression, knowing he was capable of standing there until there was nothing left of the bubbles but a ring around the tub. "I don't know what you mean," she tried confusion.

He explained. "The man you said is the father of your baby. You never told me his name."

Terrific. "Oh, you mean—" *Quick*, she thought, *think of a name*. "You mean—" The only thing between her and another embarrassing situation was a bevy of sandalwood-scented bubbles. "Bub," she said. "Bubba...Bud. His name is Bud. Bud Loofah...Loofman. Bud Loofman."

"Bud," Alex repeated, patently disbelieving. "Bud Loofman, huh? Well, I'll be damned. I thought sure you made him up."

Caught in her lie, she forced a gay denial. "Now, why would I do something like that?"

He shrugged, grinned and held her gaze long enough for the teasing to turn itself inside out. "Maybe," he said softly, seriously, "so you wouldn't have to put any faith in me."

Her heart did a startled beat, skip-beat routine as the truth of that hit home. But before she could even consider how to respond, his smile returned and he shrugged. "But I guess nothing is ever quite that simple, is it?"

Then he closed the door and Annie sat alone in the tub, watching the fragrant bubbles burst and dissipate, as if Alex had taken their reason for being with him when he left.

LOOSEY HAD PROBABLY NEVER been so clean in her whole life. She'd probably never smelled better, either. She lay, like a rug made of well-washed collie, in the middle of Annie's living room, underneath a coffee table of solid oak, on which Alex had his feet propped. He'd made a decision while he waited for Annie to dry off, dress and join him. He wasn't going home tonight. Whether she issued an invitation to stay or not, he was staying. He didn't quite know how he'd tell her, but this is where he belonged, and damn if he was going to let her order him to leave. He wanted to be with her. As close as she would allow, at least in the same house. He'd sleep on the floor if he had to. But this is where he was spending the night. He'd already phoned the ranch, chatted a minute with Willie, let her know in a roundabout way that there was no need to leave a light on. As if she didn't know that already from past times when he'd routinely missed curfew, as if she'd ever failed to leave the light on, anyway.

Now all he had to do was let Annie know he'd be bunkin' on her couch.

Loosey snored a little, moved in whatever dream she was flirting with, hit the foot of the coffee table with her cast and woke herself up. She lifted her head and looked at him, disoriented and startled.

"I know just how you feel," he told her, leaning down to scratch her head. "But it could be a whole lot worse. What if we really believed she'd name the kid Hoyt Loofman?"

Loosey's tail made a halfhearted *thump* as she yawned and laid her head against his hand. But then, like a bear alert to the smell of honey, she sat up and her tail began to thump the floor in earnest. A moment later Annie appeared in the doorway, wrapped in a fuzzy robe the same color as her eyes, her hair pulled into a wet topknot and curling about her head in a fountain of crinkly disarray. The fragrance of sandalwood and sausage pizza wafted into the room like intriguing and invisible smoke signals ahead of her. "Did you make this?" she asked, holding up a half-eaten slice of pizza.

"It didn't come out of the freezer, if that's what you mean."

"It's good. I'm impressed." She took another bite with gusto.

"It's a special recipe. Pizza à la string beans."

She considered, kept chewing, swallowed. "You did not put green beans on this pizza."

"You're right. I ground them up and put them in the crust."

Frowning, she peered at the underside of what remained of her slice. Then she shrugged. "I don't believe you, but please don't feel as if you have to prove it to me tonight, okay? I just want to sit for a while and put my feet up."

He scooted over on the sofa, patted the cushion. "Be my guest. It is, after all, your couch."

"At least you didn't let Loosey up there with you. She has this sneaky way of taking over any available lap."

"Good thing I saved my lap for you, then, huh?"

Annie rolled her eyes. "Oh, right. Like you wouldn't be squashed flat as a flapjack if I sat on you." Getting a firm grip on the sofa's rolled arm, she angled her backside down toward the cushion a little at a time. "It takes me a while, but I eventually get down."

"If you're aiming for my lap, you're gonna miss it by a quarter acre."

She dropped the rest of the way onto the cushion with a sigh of relief, and her tummy suddenly became the focal point of his attention. Leaning back, as she was, she looked bigger, rounder, more... Well, more maternal than he would ever have thought possible. Of course, he supposed, a pregnant woman was about as maternal looking as it got. Except for maybe a woman holding a baby to her breast.

Whoa. There was an image he hadn't expected. Annie and the baby. His son. The bottom dropped out of his melancholy and hit the floor running. They were having a baby. He and Annie. The magnitude of that fact flat took his breath away.

"I know," she said, misinterpreting his sigh. "I can't believe I'm this huge, either. It's not twins, though. Dr. Elizabeth ruled that possibility out months ago." Laying her hands on the swell of her belly, Annie released her breath in a rush. "Early on, after the morning sickness subsided, I thought it might be nice to have twins. You know, two for the price of one labor and delivery kind of thing. But then my waist disappeared, breathing got to be a challenge—walking and sitting, too—and I decided I was crazy to think for a second that this little guy—" she patted her tummy "—wouldn't be perfectly happy as an only child."

Alex wanted to kiss her, because he always

wanted to kiss her, but also as a sort of thank-you for putting her body through the nine-month transformation it took to bear his child. That was a pretty big sacrifice, when you thought about it. Nine months of mood swings and nausea and sitting at an angle. Nine months of weight gain and water retention and a basketball of a belly. He was both sorry for her discomfort and elated by it. But since he couldn't explain any of that to her in a way that wouldn't make him sound like Tarzan of the Apes, he guessed he wouldn't kiss her.

Leaning down, he picked up her legs, swung them onto the sofa and put her feet in his lap. He pulled off first one fuzzy house shoe, then the other and set them on the floor. Annie wiggled her toes. Her sweet-smelling, funny little toes. "I never knew you had such a foot fetish, Alex."

"Think of this second massage as a bribe."

"I thought that's what the pizza was."

"No, that was supper. This is more like an advance payment for breakfast."

Her toes went still. "As in you're bringing over doughnuts in the morning and you don't want me to grab the jelly-filled before you get a chance at it?"

He didn't want to skirt the issue. He wanted to come right out and tell her he needed to be with her, that he belonged with her. But the words wouldn't quite line up the way he wanted. "I think of breakfast more as a stick-to-your-ribs kind of meal, like Nell puts together at the Chuck Wagon. But I also think breakfast could be just a man and a woman cooking oatmeal in the kitchen after waking up together.''

There was a shift in her expression, and surprise vied with dismay in her eyes before she choked out a short laugh. "Ha, ha, very funny. Don't even try to make me believe you're sitting over there lusting for this svelte and sexy body.''

"I've been lusting after your body since seventh grade, Annie, and at no time since then have I ever not lusted for it.''

"Oh, please. Spare me the tongue-in-cheek sweet-talk, Alex.''

He met her gaze squarely, telling her in a look that he meant what he'd said, letting all the desire he felt show in his eyes. She looked away first, then brought her gaze back with an honestly confused frown as she leaned back against the sofa cushions. "What are you really after, Alex? Because I know it's not sex.''

His fingers began a circular and rhythmic massage. "Laugh at me if you want, but seeing you like this, all round and womanly, is very sexy.'' He gave her a slow and self-deprecating smile. "It was all I could do back there not to climb into the bathtub with you.''

Her laughter bordered on being just plain old nervous energy. "Quit pulling my leg.''

"I'm merely rubbing your feet, Annie, but if you want, I reckon I can give the old gams a yank or two.'' He ducked when she threw the pillow, but he didn't pick it up and toss it back. Instead he concentrated on seducing all ten of her toes and he started by kissing them. One toe at a time.

Annie stopped laughing.

She sighed, then sighed again, as he stroked the ball of her foot with his thumb, and when he teased her instep with the tip of his tongue she jerked as if it tickled, which it probably did, which only made him try it again. Softer. More of a butterfly's touch than a feathery brush of the lips. Her head drooped to rest on the back cushion and she closed her eyes. He watched her give over to the pleasure as he slid his hand to her ankle and stroked back to the sole of her foot, then followed the same path with spidery kisses and an ultrasoft touch.

She was so pretty, her creamy skin set off by the thick, dark eyelashes now resting against her cheeks and the red-gold, tousled glory of her hair. The freckles that had once been a cute dusting over her nose and cheeks had faded into a healthy complexion that blushed a vivid rose when she was embarrassed or angry. Even in the long-ago days when he fancied himself The Sundance Kid, he'd always imagined Annie as his partner, the two of them riding the valley of the Bighorn side by side, he astride a leggy sorrel, her riding a Medicine Hat pinto. Sundance and the Redhead. Alex and Annie. Even back then, they were two of a kind, outlaws of the heart, never quite belonging anywhere except with each other. That was their fortune and their fate. He knew it as well as he knew the ever-changing sunset and the persistent, Wyoming sunrise. He was pretty sure that Annie knew it, too.

Even when she was madder than a bee in molasses over something he'd done or failed to do. Even when he knew he'd disappointed her and ought to make amends but didn't. Even when she had to watch him walk away and not look back.

He didn't deserve her, not for a night or any other measure of his life. But maybe, just this once, he could persuade her to believe that he did. Maybe, just for a while, she'd turn a blind eye of faith on him and not see his flaws too clearly until morning. Maybe tonight, darkness and trust would be his allies.

Slowly, with all the tenderness in his lonely soul, he moved from the couch and knelt beside her, gathering her carefully into his arms. "Annie…?"

She turned her face to his, invitation on her lips, and before she could reconsider, he kissed her. Fiercely. Hungrily. He hadn't lied when he'd said he found her incredibly sexy at seven and a half months pregnant. The surprise was how intense the desire was to make love to her, how tight his body instantly became with wanting her…and yet how eager he was to temper that desire with restraint. When he drew the kiss to a lingering close, he loved the fact that she didn't pull away.

"Alex?" Her voice was a whisper, a breathless affirmation of pleasure, before she swallowed hard and said, "I don't think I can— I mean, sex probably isn't going to be…too great for either one of us at this…at this stage."

"Sex is always great," he said, cupping her face

in his palms, kissing her again, lightly, smiling into the frown that clouded her eyes. "But it's not what I'm after here, Annie."

"It isn't?"

He shook his head, gathered the words and the courage to ask for what he needed. "I want to stay the night," he said. "I want to sleep in the same bed, share the same blanket, hear you breathing when I wake up in the middle of the night, and have you be the first thing I see when I wake up in the morning. And I'm not talking about sex. Not because I don't want to make love to you. Not because I find your body any less desirable. I just want...need...to be with you. I want to hold you, caress you, kiss you and stay close to you all the night long. I know it must sound like a crazy idea to you, but—"

"Okay."

"—it's really not so..." He stopped talking. Stopped his runaway explanation. Stopped breathing. "'Okay?' As in forget the jelly doughnuts and bring out the carton of oatmeal?"

She laughed, sounding as breathless as he felt. "As long as I don't have to eat the oatmeal and as long as you're not expecting a night of unmitigated passion, I'd sort of appreciate the company."

He couldn't believe it. She said yes. "Yes?" he repeated, his heart in his throat. "You mean it?"

She bobbed her head in a funny little nod, stroked his jaw with the back of her hand. "Sometimes, Alex—not all the time, but once in a while—it is that simple.''

He kissed her then. Gently. Passionately. And very, very thankfully.

Chapter Nine

Annie couldn't sleep. She lay in the dark, delighting in the feel of the warm man curled along her backside like a familiar dream. She knew he was awake, too. Could tell by the shallow, sometimes uneven, depths of his breathing that he was as aware of her as she was of him…and just as determined not to disturb her. She wondered what he was thinking, but didn't want to ask. What if he told her he was going through the motions of training Koby in his head? What if he was remembering some faraway place where she'd never been and to which he wanted to return? What if his thoughts were a million miles from hers, and getting farther away by the second? What if tomorrow morning was the day he would leave?

She had come very close to telling him he was right. That she'd made up a father for her baby because she didn't trust Alex to take the responsibility that was rightfully his. Of course he knew she was lying. She hadn't tried all that hard to convince him otherwise, which was a lie in itself.

What had she hoped for? That he'd step up to the plate and force the issue instead of occasionally nudging her to admit the truth? That he'd declare this child to be his, a McIntyre by genetics and the law, and vow he would never leave her or their son as long as he lived? Alex didn't make promises like that; she knew from experience. And to believe he'd changed now, simply because he was here beside her...?

Well, good intentions aside, bottom line, she didn't trust Alex to stay with her. Baby or no baby.

So that left the only thing she'd ever really had in the first place. Now. Today. This moment...with no guarantee of more to follow. It wasn't all she wanted, but she'd take it and be glad for it. And she wouldn't ask him for more by telling him the baby was his. In his heart he knew the truth. The choice, when he finally made it, would be his own, uninfluenced by what she hoped for or wanted.

He moved and slipped his arm around her, hesitating when his hand touched the bulky, unyielding roundness of her tummy. She closed her fingers over his and drew his palm down across the cotton nightshirt that covered her, holding it flat against her stomach. It took a moment, maybe more, before she felt him relax. "Know what I was thinking?" he said, his breath stirring the hair at the back of her head.

"How great cold pizza would taste right now?" she whispered back, wishing the night would never, ever end.

"No." She could hear the disgust in the single

syllable. "I was thinking about the night you got so mad at your uncle you decided to run away. Remember?"

Remember being mad at Uncle Dex? Vaguely. Remember the first time Alex made love to her? Like it was yesterday. "Mmm-hmm," she murmured. "It was the summer after high school graduation and the only summer I qualified to work as a counselor at the Summer Arts Camp near Cheyenne, but Uncle Dex said he needed me to stay home and help him at the clinic. I was so mad I was ready to give up my college scholarship just to get away from him."

"He wasn't open to compromise and neither were you. So you barebacked that walleyed cayuse he called a saddle horse out to Silver Horn Lake and he called me to go fetch you."

"He called you?" she asked, surprised.

"He figured I'd know where to find you and that you'd be more apt to listen to me than him, anyway."

She frowned. "I never knew that."

"I know. At the time, I was in the mood to be your hero. I wanted you to believe I just sensed you were in trouble and knew you needed me. I wanted to be there for you." He paused. "In truth, I was just scared because I was getting ready to leave for Florida and I was afraid you'd fall in love with somebody else and well, the long and short of it was, I took advantage of the situation that night and I've always felt guilty about that."

She remembered pretty clearly exactly which

one of them had been the aggressor—and it hadn't
been Alex. "As I recall, Alex, it took a whole lot
of persuasion to get you to 'take advantage' of me
and I certainly have no regrets about it. I was going
to get in trouble that night, Alex, one way or another. I was primed for it."

"And I was right there to make sure you did."

"And I've always believed you saved me from
making a really big mistake that night. Alex?"

"Yes?"

"Can you feel that?" She moved his hand
lower, to the place where the baby moved in a
ripple of sensation just below the quickening beat
of her heart. "He's changing position."

Behind her, she heard Alex swallow hard and
knew she couldn't have peeled his hand away from
her stomach just then if she'd tried. "I feel him,"
he said in a voice that might have been struck by
lightning for all its awed, whispery excitement.
"He's moving around."

She laughed softly. "Yes, he is."

"Does it hurt?"

"No. Sometimes it's a little bit uncomfortable,
but I just think about how cramped his space is
getting in there and remind myself that there are a
lot of things in life that are worth some discomfort." She turned over so she could look into his
eyes. "Like you, for instance."

Alex levered up onto his elbow, but kept his
hand on her stomach as the baby rolled again.
"Me?"

"You. There are times—like tonight and the

clinic visit—when I could happily strangle you with both hands. Then there are times—like the night at Silver Horn Lake and now—when I'm just happy to have you in my life.''

''But, Annie, I—''

''Shhhh,'' she cautioned, not wanting him to spoil the moment with words. Meaningless words. She didn't want to know his plans for tomorrow. She didn't want to think too far ahead. She just wanted now. This moment, when the three of them were—whether Alex realized it or not—a family.

KOBY NICKERED SOFTLY as Alex approached the stall. Probably happier about the smell of bran mash than because he wanted company. ''Hi, ya, fella.'' Alex opened the stall door and slipped inside, patting the velvety, dark nose that was already zeroing in on breakfast.

The leg looked better every day, the swelling receding faster than either Alex or Annie had expected. Which was a good sign. Maybe he'd add a few extra minutes to their exercise time today, see if the horse showed any sign of discomfort.

Discomfort, Annie had said last night. *Some things are worth a little discomfort*. She was quick to warn him not to rush Koby back into training. He knew she was right, of course. But the temptation was still there. He'd staked so much on winning the futurity, invested so heavily in the belief that this horse would make his reputation and his future, put all his eggs in this one equine basket.

Never for a second considering what would happen
if Koby was injured or just flat didn't perform well.

"Some trainer I am." He ran a practiced eye
over the animal, taking satisfaction in the sturdy
musculature, in the sleek symmetry of a superb
athlete, in the competitive spirit in his huge, dark
eyes. Alex wasn't wrong about Kodiak Blue. No
matter what his brothers thought. There were times
when a man had to trust his gut, and this was one
of them. He'd wait out the month, rein in his im-
patience to work Koby, hide his very real worry
that all his plans, everything he'd worked so hard
for, could wind up amounting to nothing. If Koby
didn't recover fully from his injury, if he didn't
train well afterward, if he wasn't ready for the futurity at the end of December... Well, Matt and
Jeff wouldn't want to proceed with the training and
breeding programs at the S-J.

Even if they encouraged him to revamp his orig-
inal plan and approach the whole idea from a different slant, Alex knew this was his one and only
shot. He had to go in a winner or not do the job
at all. Implementing a training program without the
full confidence of his brothers and with his own
confidence shaken... Well, the whole idea would
have three strikes against it before he even got it
started. He hadn't thought it through before, all
that might happen if Koby didn't compete and win
the futurity. He'd never even considered what
could go wrong and what would happen if it did.
He had that much faith in this horse. But suddenly,
last night, when he'd felt the baby—his son—

move under his hand, the future took on a scary cast. If his plans fell through, then what did he have to offer Annie and the baby? No backup strategy. No if-this-doesn't-work, we'll-do-this-instead options. No second choices. Nothing except more disappointment. And that he simply would not do. Not to Annie who tried so hard to make him out as her hero.

The feed bucket clanked as Koby nosed it against the boards and Alex shrugged off the mantle of worry. It was too late to rethink his decisions, too late to go back and take a less risky, more conservative approach to launching a business. He had things to prove between now and then. He wanted Annie to have plumbing that worked, an automatic dishwasher, a pantry stocked full of groceries, a nursery furnished with everything a little fellow might need to get his life started. Annie would be delivering his son around the beginning of the new year, the start of the new century, but hopefully not at the same time he was risking their future on a cutting horse. He had to be here for the baby's birth. He had to ride Koby in the futurity events. But for now, all he could do was hope the two events wouldn't coincide and prepare as best he could for both. The S-J provided a good income for all of them on a yearly basis, so there was no excuse for a McIntyre to be born needing anything that money could buy. That much, at least, he could do for Annie. And his son.

"I'll be back later," he said to Koby, who paid next to no attention. "Can't skip your exercise, now can we? Too many dreams riding on you, big guy. Too many pie-in-the-sky dreams.''

"A DISHWASHER?" Annie had come home from the clinic to find Alex under her sink and a brand-spanking-new dishwasher installed where once she'd had a nice-size cabinet. "You put in a dishwasher?"

He slid out from under the sink, so pleased with himself, it was impossible not to smile in return. "Yep," he said. "Had a little help from Ray with getting the pipes all hooked up properly, but I did the carpentry part all by my lonesome. What d'ya think?"

"It's very—" what did one say about a dishwasher that would be considered a compliment "—shiny."

"I can change the panel, if you want. Make it black instead of white. Look inside. It's stainless steel. Plus, there's a rack you can raise or lower which will accommodate any size baby bottle. Handy, huh?"

Annie admired the stainless steel interior, examined the adjustable rack, raised and lowered it. "Very handy," she agreed.

He nodded with—amazingly—even greater enthusiasm. "There's also a built-in heat sensor for the water so you won't have to worry about sterilizing anything. It'll get plenty hot enough, and you can put the bottle caps and nipples in that little compartment—" he pointed out the compartment with a snap-down lid "—and rest easy that nothing is going to fall down on the heating elements and melt.''

"I would have worried about that,'' she said with wry good humor.

"Well, now you won't have to.''

She'd never seen him quite so taken with one of his own accomplishments and only wished he'd asked her before he'd bought the thing and installed it. Not that she'd have said no. Just that she would have liked to know he was tearing up her kitchen before he'd already gone and done it. "It'll be a big help, Alex. Thank you.''

"You're welcome. Once the baby comes, you're not going to want to be spending any time washing dishes by hand.''

No, indeed. "I was thinking I'd just order a month of pizzas in advance, use paper plates, plastic forks, disposable bottles. You know, simplify suppertime around here.'' She laughed at the furrows of frown gathering across his brow. "I'm teasing, Alex. I love the dishwasher. Really. But where are we going to put all the stuff that was in that cabinet?''

"Don't worry.'' Wrench in hand, he scooted back under the sink. "I've got an idea.''

A WEEK LATER, her back porch had undergone a transformation, given up its identity as a cluttered, screened-in, added-on-as-an-afterthought porch and become a closed-in laundry room, complete with washer, dryer, oversize pantry, and enough spare footage left over to hold a plant stand. With plants. A Boston fern, a Norfolk pine, two African violets, and a good-size cactus plant. All looking healthy and happy under the ultraviolet glow of a grow-lamp. Complements of Mr. Handy, himself. It was wonderfully warm in the new room, too, courtesy of the new central heat and air-conditioning system installed in a remarkably rushed, rush job by Ray Shields's son-in-law, Tom Stragge, who was, if possible, a bigger procrastinator than Ray himself.

"Mmm," Annie said after Alex finished giving her the grand tour and explaining the gyrations he'd gone through to make sure the project was completed in record time. "Looks like I'm in your debt again, Alex."

His expression went from elated to worried in a split second. "You don't like it. What's wrong with it? The color? 'Cause I can repaint it, Annie. It doesn't have to stay like this. But that yellow paint was left over from the baby's room and I thought it would brighten this whole back porch room so—"

"The color's fine." She felt bad for not being able to work up the enthusiasm he obviously had expected. But it was her house. And he hadn't asked her opinion. He'd just torn into remodeling as if the place was Humpty-Dumpty and it was up to Alex to put it back together again. "It's wonderful," she said, pushing forth a smile. "Really. I couldn't have planned it any better myself." Which was an accurate statement, if not exactly what she was feeling.

But it seemed to make him happy and, truly, that was enough to make her happy, too.

BABY FURNITURE. A whole roomful of it. A honey-colored oak crib with comforter and bumper pads in a rodeo print. A changing table of the same hon-eyed wood. Also a chest of drawers and a little nightstand. A lamp, with rodeo print shade, and a grouping of bright pictures featuring cowboys on bucking horses for the walls. It was everything she'd lusted after in the *Ranchman's* catalog...and then some.

"Well?" Alex asked, standing behind her in the doorway of the nursery. "Is this everything you wanted?"

Emotion choked her and she didn't know whether she wanted to burst into tears or yell at him. Whether to explain that his generosity was suffocating her or that everything she wanted was simply him. Just him. Not once in the week since he'd started staying with her had he said so much as "boo" about the future. He hadn't said he'd stay until the baby was born. He hadn't said he wouldn't. And she didn't see any way she could ask.

The way he was taking charge of fixing every-thing in her life made her nervous. She'd wanted to share this special time with him, not have him scout the path ahead like it was his job to keep the Indians from attacking the wagon train. She sensed that he was keeping busy as much for his own sake as for hers and the baby's. She knew him well enough to understand this encounter with domesticity was a novelty and that she shouldn't expect it to last forever.

But right there was her trouble. Because forever was exactly what her foolish heart was beginning to believe she could have.

"It's perfect, Alex," she said, even though experience warned her it wasn't.

SUNDAY DINNER with the McIntyres was a mixed blessing. Annie, hesitant to accept Alex's persistent invitation, wound up going and having a wonderful time being with Josie. Willie, too, had advice and anecdotes galore for the two mothers-in-waiting. The three women cleaned the kitchen after the meal, tossed around ideas for the baby contest and generally stirred up a batch of shared laughter and female bonding. But joining the men in the living room afterward quickly put a stop to that. The tension in the room was as ripe as a week-old banana, and it didn't take much to discern that the brothers had been exchanging a few disagreeable words. Or that Alex was at the pivotal center of the exchange, either. His expression, shadowed and somber, told Annie all she needed to know.

Justin brightened considerably when the women walked in and Josie frowned at her three brothers in turn. "Anybody up for a friendly game of Scrabble?"

Jeff groaned. "Not now, Jo. Even though I could easily beat your boots off."

"Since when?" Josie wrinkled her nose at her middle brother and turned to Alex. "What about you, 'Lex? You know how to spell *yippie-ki-yi-ay?*"

The mood shifted as the McIntyre men gave in to three almost-identical smiles. Annie wondered if in the coming year she'd see that same smile on the face of her son.

"When I was seven or so," Josie explained to Annie and Justin, "these yahoos taught me how to play Scrabble and I loved it. I mean really, really loved it."

"Only because Mom made us let you win all the time."

Josie stuck out her tongue at her oldest brother. "I won because I could outspell all three of you without stopping to blink."

"You won," Alex added his two cents worth, "because you were the baby and a *girl.*"

"And," Jeff picked up the explanation, "because we pretended we were paying attention to what we were spelling. The sorry truth is, Jo, we hated Scrabble."

The two older brothers nodded in agreement, and Matt added, "Knowing we had to let you win took the challenge right out of it."

"Bull patootie," Josie declared. "I beat you all fair and square every time."

"Did not." Alex argued, grinning.

"Did, too."

"I'll swan," Willie said, settling back in her favorite overstuffed armchair. "Will you young'uns stop fussing and let Josie explain to Justin and Annie how she got in trouble over *yippie-ki-yi-ay?*"

"I hold all of them—" Josie indicated all brothers with a nod "—equally responsible, although it was Alex who told me I could get extra points using genuine Cherokee Indian words."

Justin started laughing right then. "Did you *know* any Cherokee words, Alex?"

"No, but Jo didn't know that. Jeff and Matt came up with a bunch of them, but I made up the infamous *yippie-ki-yi-ay.*" He cleared his throat and smiled easily and especially at Annie. "I told her it was pronounced the way she'd always heard it, but spelled according to the Cherokee alphabet, with accent marks and everything, it turned out to look remarkably like *yippie-kiss-my*—uh, let's substitute *behind,* as I've learned a little tact since then."

Justin lost it and burst out laughing. As did Matt, Jeff and Alex. Josie watched them all with both exasperation and adoration, before she rolled her eyes and shared a "Men!" look with Annie. "Now, you understand why Mom and Dad always loved me best." She shook her head and continued, "I went right to school ready to impress Miss Westner, my elderly and very proper second-grade teacher, with my new knowledge of the Cherokee language, and when it came time to write sentences using the week's spelling words, I dutifully penned a beauty." She paused, then delivered her sentence with enthusiasm, "'Miss Westner has a boyfriend

who rides and sings *yippie-ki-yi-ay*.' Spelled the
way Alex taught me, of course.''

The men laughed harder and the last of the tension ebbed away, forgotten in their enjoyment of
past brotherly crimes. Annie caught the look ex-
changed between Josie and Willie. Mission accom-
plished. The family gathering was once more full
of shared memories and laughter.

Annie had missed out on all this. Or if she'd
ever had a true sense of her family, she'd long
since lost the ability to recall it. She wanted her
son to share in his heritage, too, she realized.
Which meant she would have to claim it for him.
Which meant she would have to tell Alex what he
already knew—what probably every single person
in this room already suspected.

And yet, in the telling, she would put Alex in
another clash with his nemesis.

She wondered if he was ready to spell *responsibility*.

"LOOK AT THESE!" Alex held up a pair of tiny
denim jeans. "And this." Next up was a miniature
set of chaps—cute as the dickens, although, in
Annie's opinion, completely useless. "Where do
people find this stuff?"

Under strict orders to relax, Annie sat in the
carved, wooden rocker and watched Alex put away
the receiving blankets, sheets, towels and miscellaneous baby gifts received just that afternoon at
her baby shower. "There's a specialty store in Cas-
per with nothing but Western wear for infants and

children. Plus there must be a million catalogs floating around with novelty items of one sort or another.'' She sighed, smiled, felt particularly weary on this cold Sunday afternoon at the end of October. ''With all the attention the baby contest is generating for predictions on when all these new little cowboys and cowgirls will arrive, the town has gone baby crazy. Do you realize there's a baby shower every weekend between now and the middle of December? I'm just glad mine was one of the first. Josie suggested one huge baby shower for everyone, but Willie and Nell thought that'd be too much work and not as much fun as individual and separate occasions, and since they're basically in charge of planning the showers...''

Alex rummaged through a stack of diapers. ''I knew I saw these while you were unwrapping packages.'' He held up a diaper pin set—plastic cowboys on plastic bucking broncs at the ends of two large safety pins. ''Who would ever have thought somebody would pay good money for these? I should have gone into marketing,'' he said. ''Like Jeff.''

''Oh, right. As if you didn't make a hundred-and-eighty-degree turn every time Jeff or Matt expressed so much as a passing interest in a career field. For a while, I thought you'd have no choice but to be a plumber or a chef if you were going to avoid any overlapping interest.''

''A plumber or a chef, huh? That'd be quite a stretch for a guy who was all but born on a horse...and born a McIntyre, to boot.''

"You've always been more outlaw than conformist, Alex. There have even been times when I expected you to sell out your interest in the S-J and never look back."

"There were times when I thought about it, once when I even talked to my dad about it."

"Hoping that he'd give you a shot at running the ranch instead of Matt?"

That struck a nerve. Annie saw the idea hit home, saw the flash of regret in his expression. "That was never an option for me and I knew it," he said in a tone that was too offhand, too blithe to conceal the undertone of disappointment. "I never expected...never wanted that kind of responsibility."

The words hung there, pulled down by the weight of the denial. "You could have worked with Matt," she said, wanting him to see that he'd had a choice. "I think your dad always hoped you'd take an interest in ranch management."

He shrugged, smoothed the wrinkles on a folded square of baby blanket. "Matt had that job pretty well sewed up before I came along. Which worked out for the best, anyway. Gave me the opportunity to be the explorer of the family."

But she could tell by his tone he didn't think "explorer" was much of an occupation next to "rancher." "Have you ever considered the idea that you've made choices Matt and Jeff probably wish they could have made?"

"Now there's a far-fetched notion. My brothers were born to carry on the McIntyre legacy, Annie.

They knew from birth what choices they should make, and they're sure as hell not envious of mine.''

"You're as much an heir of that legacy as either of your brothers. You were born a McIntyre, too, Alex. The difference is you've just never been able to figure out what that means to you."

He put the jeans, chaps and rodeo diaper pins in the top drawer of the changing table and a stack of one-piece sleepers in the bottom drawer of the honey-oak chest. She idly made a mental note to switch them later and set the chair to a gentle rocking, which in the silence, was soothing. His voice, when it came, drifted to her through a dreamy haze. "What is the McIntyre name going to mean to our son, Annie?"

She blinked, startled from the moment's lethargy and by the unexpected question. "Our son?" she repeated, not sure what he was angling for.

He stopped what he was doing, straightened, squared his shoulders and faced her, looking tall, handsome and so very resolute. "That's what I said, Annie. *Our* son. The one growing beneath your heart at this very moment."

She'd known this talk was coming, had fooled herself into thinking she could choose the time and place, had thought she'd be ready. But here it was—and she was scared and not ready at all. "Ever since you've been back," she said, keeping her voice light, noncommittal, "you've seemed pretty anxious to take responsibility for this little guy."

"And you've seemed pretty eager to keep me from it."

She rested her hands on her tummy and eased her way carefully, lightly, into the words. "It isn't that..."

"Easy?" He filled in for her when she paused. "Isn't that what you were about to say, Annie? Funny thing is I don't recall asking you to make it easy. I only asked you to tell me the truth."

The baby inside her stirred restlessly, perhaps sensing his parents had just taken aim at his future and each other. "Truth, Alex? The truth is you walked back into my life as if you'd just walked out the day before, and jumped to a big conclusion. Then you set about insisting I confirm it." Old irritations stirred, stretched, sharpened their claws. "And you didn't seem all that interested in what I had to say about it, either."

"Oh, come on, Annie. I'm not some dumb cowpoke who can't track a wagon through a mud puddle. Your story was tied up in knots from the beginning. A man you were in school with—perfectly believable. A fellow student who spent years getting a veterinary degree so he could join the Peace Corps and go to Africa? Admirable, but a little on the iffy side truthwise. A man named Bud Loofman?" He shook his head. "That has 'made up' written all over it."

"I'll be sure to tell him you think so."

"You do that, just as soon as you locate an address for him. I'm not blind, either, Annie.

There're no pictures, no postcards, no trace of his existence in your life.''

She was angry now because he didn't see what was so clearly in front of him. Her. Alone. No pictures, no postcards, no promises. No mementos of him...save one. "And how is that different from you, Alex?"

"It's my baby, Annie. Be honest. Admit it."

"Why? So you can carry a picture of a little boy in your wallet and show him off to your friends? So there'll be someone else whose birthday you can never quite remember?"

He looked away, brought his gaze back to bear steadily on hers. "You may as well know this now, Annie. The Midwestern Cutting Horse Futurity in Denver is three full days, startin' December 29. The finals will be New Year's Eve. I'm riding Koby there that night."

Of course. It was probably written in some book of ill-fated lovers somewhere that Alex wouldn't be around when his son was born. No point in even asking which event held more importance in his eyes. No point in speculating whether the baby would come before or after the three-day event. Alex had made his choice already.

Suddenly all her own disappointments were mixed up with her protective instincts, and she lashed out at Alex in anger because he'd left her before and because he was getting ready to do it again. "You do what you have to do, Alex. But you're not getting a walk-on part in my son's life. You're not going to pick and choose when you'll show up to be a father and when something else takes priority. You're not going to come within breaking distance of his heart." She swallowed, dismayed by her outburst, by the pent-up emotional residue of too many goodbyes. "You're not going to hurt him, Alex, because I won't let you. This is my son. Mine. Not yours. Do you hear me? He is not your son." She had never seen him look so pale, so stricken, and was instantly, genuinely sorry to have hurt him. "I'm sorry, but—"

"Sorry?" he repeated. "No, Annie. I think that's my line. I thought I was finally getting this responsibility thing right, helping you prepare for the baby's arrival, fixing up the place—nesting, I guess some folks would call it—taking care of his future by doing what I know how to do best. Training horses. But apparently I just don't *get* it." He smiled without a trace of humor. "Guess the joke's on me. I finally come home thinking I know what I want to do with the rest of my life, and what d'ya know? All the mistakes I thought I wasn't making have been right here all along, just waiting to spit in my eye."

He strode purposefully to the doorway, and Annie tried to think of something to say that would stop him. But what was there left to say except goodbye?

Hand on the door frame, he paused but didn't look back. "I appreciate your concern for the baby. But if he is a McIntyre, don't think I won't fight you to make sure he has everything that is rightfully his. And part of that is me, Annie. Bad as my influence may be, part of his heritage is me. Whether you or anyone else has any faith in my ability to be a good father, I intend to make sure my son knows he has one. That's a promise.''

His footsteps resounded through the house like the terrible pounding of her heartbeat. *Thud-thud-thud.*

She heard the back door slam, and then there was nothing but the silence.

Chapter Ten

Annie closed the door, shutting out the worried animal sounds in the clinic's waiting room, and looked at the telephone on her desk. She did not want to make this call. She did not want to hear the answer to her question.

But it wasn't going to get any easier, so she took a deep breath, picked up the receiver and dialed the number.

"Josie?" She leaned against the edge of the desk. "It's Annie."

The pause was so slight, she probably would have missed it if she hadn't been so keyed up and wired for trouble. "Hi," Josie said brightly. "What's up?"

"Typical Monday," she answered. "Genevieve thinks the clinic's overhead is eating into her retirement funds, so she's double booked appointments all week."

"Put the extra money aside and retire her," Josie advised. "You'll be dead tired for a while, but after that, you won't have to put up with her everlasting bossiness."

"I've tried to fire her, but she only laughs." Annie managed a rueful smile, then realized no one was there to see her effort, anyway. "Besides, she's probably right. The clinic wouldn't last two weeks without her. Uncle Dex has reluctantly agreed to work for six weeks after the baby's born, but he won't do it unless Genevieve's there to run the place. So I'm going to have to depend on her help pretty desperately after the first of the year."

"Can you believe it?" Josie's natural exuberance gushed over the phone lines. "Two months from now, it'll be time for the babies to come. I hope they're all born at the exact same second after midnight on December 31!"

"Don't let Dr. Elizabeth hear you say that. Imagine our little three-bed maternity ward overflowing with women in labor." Annie shuddered at the thought. "Plus, think what that would do to our contest. There'd be cries of a rigged contest all over the place."

Josie laughed. "Mainly from the men, I'll bet. I imagine every one of the women will be more than happy if they miss the New Year's deadline by a week or more."

"Only if it's on the December side. I sure don't want to be still waiting for this baby a week into January."

"You're absolutely right. I'm already so anxious to hold my son or daughter I can hardly stand it."

"Still don't want to know which one you're

having?'' Annie imagined Josie's head shaking from side to side in an emphatic no.

"We'd rather be surprised at the last minute. I sort of think it's a boy, but Willie is adamant I'm having a girl. She says she's had enough of rambunctious boys for a while." Josie sighed happily. "As if I couldn't give birth to a girl child who would give a whole new meaning to *rambunctious*."

"A *yippie-ki-yi-ay* kind of girl?"

Josie laughed. "Exactly that kind."

Annie gathered her courage and took the plunge. "I was wondering, Josie, if…you've talked to Alex today?"

The slight hesitation made the coming answer very clear. "Not exactly."

Hanging on to a thin straw of hope, Annie held the phone tighter to her ear and waited.

"According to Willie's account of events, it seems he and Matt had a long, and not entirely cordial, discussion late last night and then this morning…. He's gone." Josie sighed. "I'm sorry, Annie. I hoped he had, at least, said goodbye to you."

He had. He'd said it very plainly. "Well, Alex never has been big on lingering farewells."

"No," Josie agreed. "I suppose it's a little late in the game to start expecting him to change, huh? What about the horse?"

"Missing in action. The mammoth horse trailer, too." Annie swallowed the urge to cry. "Both gone when I woke up this morning." She hadn't slept much, but enough so that she'd missed watching Alex drive off.

"And the dog?"

Loosey, thankfully, he'd left behind. "Looks like she's mine for the duration."

"You were right not to tell him he's the father of your baby, Annie. Much as I hate to say this about my own brother, if he can't even take responsibility for a dog, he has no business with a child." There was a funny little gasp from Josie's end of the line, then a quickly phrased apology. "I can't believe I just said that, Annie. That was so completely...tactless."

"Josie, I've got to go. Genevieve's outside the door, arguing with Dinah about something. We'll talk later, okay?" But she didn't wait for Josie's agreement. Annie just hung up the phone, without saying goodbye, and closed her eyes to fight back a flood of tears.

She'd known Alex was leaving last night. Some sixth sense called experience had been telling her since the day he got back that he would go. What else was all the money he'd spent on the house—all the fixing up, the miscellaneous necessities he'd bought for the baby—if not a way of letting her know that, once again, he wouldn't be around for an important event in her life? So why did she feel as if the proverbial rug had just been jerked out from under her feet? If she'd expected Alex to leave from the second he returned, why was she now surprised that he had?

"Doc Annie? You in there?" The inquiry was

followed by a tap at the door and then Genevieve herself. "I've put Ol' Lady Green and her *purrsian* cat in exam room three, but you don't need to be in a big hurry to get in there. It'll do that old woman some good to have to spend ten minutes alone with that sorry excuse for a feline. Never saw such a mean-tempered cat in my whole life. Must be the company she keeps." Genevieve started out, pulling the door to as she went. "Oh, by the way, that McIntyre boy left a check in the mailbox for boarding his horse, even though he'd already paid for the whole month of October. Wrote on the check, 'For damages.' You'll need to check that out. See if there's repairs to do. Can't think why else he'd write that on there. Musta been in a hurry, that boy. Guess he had places to go."

The door shut, either because Genevieve hadn't noticed the tears running down Annie's cheeks or because she had and was, belatedly, developing some sensitivity. Not that Annie cared. She was too involved in the realization that she'd been wrong about Alex all along. It wasn't his lack of responsibility he was always running from, it was her lack of faith in him. It was her inability to trust him to be responsible and to do the right thing for her, for himself, for their son. No one wanted to give Alex the benefit of the doubt. Not Matt. Or Jeff. Not even Josie. And now, Annie, too, had failed to believe in him when he needed her to the most. If she'd been halfway sensitive to his needs all these years, she'd have invested her love not with the belief that he'd always be leaving her behind, but with the confident expectation that he'd always be coming back. Now, too late, she understood. Now, when he was gone for good.

For damages.

Annie wondered just how much he thought a broken heart was worth.

ALEX SPENT THANKSGIVING DAY working Koby. It was the same way he spent every day. In fact, life on the Keyline Ranch in Doversville, Texas, was nothing if not predictable. Just what Alex wanted. Nothing but predictable, exhausting, climb-into-bed-at-night-too-tired-to-think routine. He couldn't afford thoughts of Wyoming and Annie. He couldn't afford to imagine how easily life there went on without him. He had to focus on one thing now. Koby and the cutting futurity. The event that would make or break his career before it really began. His future rode the fence until Koby had won or lost. The horse and the work and the contest had to be everything to him because, right now, he had nothing else.

Afterward…well, he'd either go home in triumph or defeat and, one way or another, his family would take him in. Annie, on the other hand, might not.

He went over those three weeks he'd spent with her on many a midnight when he couldn't fight off the melancholy of being so far away from her. And it always came back to one issue. He'd disappointed her. The one thing he'd promised himself he'd never do. He'd made sure he couldn't let her down. After all, if he made no promises, offered no commitments, gave no undying vows of love-forever-after, then she couldn't reasonably be disappointed if he failed to measure up. It had been his motto since some long-ago moment when he became aware of all the expectations resting on his little boy's shoulders. Running had seemed the simplest way to avoid disappointing the people who loved him, the best and easiest way to avoid out-and-out failure.

Well, he was face-to-face with it now. Koby had recovered completely from the bowed tendon. He seemed happy enough to be back at the familiar surroundings of the Keyline Ranch, where Alex had trained him last summer. The Keyline was small. Minuscule, next to the seemingly endless acreage of the S-J. But in addition to having a grade-A training facility, the Keyline's main asset was the owner, Benny Colter, who didn't care where Alex came from or what his name was. He cared, first, last, and always, about horses. And, once in a while, about the people who rode them.

"He's just not interested," Alex complained after a particularly disappointing session with Koby. "Ever since the injury, he seems to have lost his edge."

Benny climbed down from his usual perch, ringside, swiped a hand over his sparsely covered gray head and put his hat back on. "There's nothing wrong with your horse, son. There's somethin' lost in you."

Alex tasted the truth in that…and the fear. "Nothin' I can't get along without."

"Maybe you can and maybe you can't. Not for me to say. But until you decide which it is, don't go blamin' your horse. He ain't changed. He's still all he ever was." The old man turned, started to walk away, turned back. "So are you, boy. So are you."

"I can't just give up and go back there empty-handed," Alex said, admitting to himself that that was exactly what he wanted to do. He wanted to go home to Annie, to these last days of waiting for the baby to come. He no longer cared if she wouldn't admit the baby was his. He no longer cared whether or not it was. He would be Daddy—a good, dependable, always-there daddy—to Annie's child, either way. If she'd give him one little snip of a chance. If she'd just allow him one more chance to prove how much he loved her. If she'd only believe that proving himself in a contest of his peers was in her best interest, too.

After the futurity, he'd fly home. Win or lose, he'd be there New Year's Day. Winner or loser, he was going home to stay.

THE SMELL OF SAWDUST and cows, competition and excitement was a heady mix as Alex rode out of the arena. Koby had never been better and was far and away the leader going into the final round tomorrow night. In the preliminary events, he'd performed like the superb athlete he was, and Alex should have been busting out all over in prideful smiles. But his thoughts were miles away with Annie and the child who was still—Josie had passed along the information just that morning— waiting to be born. It was a tribute even to Kodiak Blue's now-undeniable talent that he'd worked like a professional while his rider and trainer sat back and paid a deplorable lack of interest.

Swinging down from the saddle in the stable area, Alex caught Benny's eye and knew his lack of enthusiasm hadn't escaped notice. "This is a fine animal," Benny said. "Better'n you deserve."

Alex nodded. "He's going to win."

"Yep. Isn't that what you trained him to do?"

"I've worked him hard for it," Alex agreed. "Pushed him to be his best. And now..." He swallowed hard. It wasn't easy to give up a long-held dream. "I'm about to hand him a big disappointment." He patted Koby's sweaty neck. "I'm leaving. Going home to Wyoming. Today. First flight I can get out of here. I'll walk if I have to, but I'm going to be there with Annie when my son's born."

Benny nodded, offered Koby an approving nose rub. "You could probably get more'n you paid for this fella, if you were of a mind to sell him. Couple of people have approached me with the question just today. 'Course, you'd get a lot more if he could go on and take the top prize tomorrow."

Alex didn't think he could bear to part with this horse. On the other hand, he wasn't looking forward to taking him home without the championship trophy, either. Matt and Jeff wouldn't see much difference from withdrawing the horse from the competition and just plain losing. They still wouldn't have any faith in Koby. Or in Alex, for that matter. "I don't know what I want to do with him," he said, then stopped, realizing that he did know. He knew exactly what he wanted. "No, on second thought, tell anyone who asks that he's not for sale. He'll be standing stud at the S-J Ranch, if they're interested. And if they're not... Well, he's proved himself to me and that's good enough."

"You'd best get to the airport if you're gonna make it home before that baby comes." Benny took the reins from Alex. "I'll take care of withdrawing your name. I'll even truck the horse to your ranch for you in a few days. Consider it a baby gift."

Alex felt like hugging the old man, but settled for shaking his hand. "Thanks, Benny. I'll save you a bubble-gum cigar."

"Just don't name the kid after me, and we'll consider it a swap. Now, get the hell home, would ya?"

Alex got.

LOOSEY PERKED HER EARS, got up, wagged her tail and barked once, sharply, as if assuring Annie that she was on guard and unafraid. Which was a good thing, because Annie was too pregnant to do anything except recline on the sofa with her feet up. At least, she thought her feet were up. She'd given up even trying to see them over the huge, round barrel of her belly. How an infant could take up so much space in a body was infinitely mysterious, but Annie was past finding any part of this nine-month drama awe inspiring. She was simply weary all the way to her toenails and weepy all the way to her eyelashes. "It's just Uncle Dex," she told the collie, whose tail was still swinging with the even beat of a metronome. "Come to take care of the large animals."

She'd hated to ask for help, but was glad now she had. It was dark already on this next-to-last-day of December, and January's clipping chill was thick in the outside air. Annie had turned over the arduous, more physical aspects of her job to Uncle Dex back in November, when Dr. Elizabeth advised her to rest more and worry less. He hadn't complained as much as Annie had expected. He'd even started stopping by the house every evening to check on her. He could say all he wanted that he was just coming in to warm his hands or to take a bite of supper with her, but she knew it was merely his way of making sure she was okay.

There had been several folks checking on her during the past two months. Nell brought her left-overs from the café once in a while—healthy choices, of course. Willie came by for lunch every Thursday, rain or shine. She said it was her market day and she wanted to check on Loosey, but Annie knew and appreciated the true reason. Not to mention the homemade pizza she insisted on sticking in Annie's freezer for later. Josie called often, usually with ideas for the contest, but generally worked the conversation around to comparing pregnancies at one point or another. She never mentioned Alex, probably waiting for Annie to do so. But Annie never did. Even Alex's brothers called a few times on the pretext of either needing or paying for veterinary supplies at the ranch, but it wasn't hard to decipher their generous intentions.

Everything was ready for the baby. Annie had enrolled and completed Dr. Elizabeth's classes in natural childbirth, even though she'd gone alone. She could have asked Willie or Nell, she supposed, to be her coach. Or even Genevieve, but somehow Annie felt reluctant to have anyone with her. She wanted Alex, and since she couldn't have his hand to hold, she'd prefer to go the distance alone.

Her biggest worry lately seemed to be going into labor when Uncle Dex was around—something she did not want to happen. Much as she appreciated his gruff concern, she didn't think she could bear to have him pacing the halls of the hospital, fussing at anyone who crossed his path, while she was…well, doing what women did while having a baby. It wasn't the pain she thought about so much as having no one to hold her hand when it got bad. *If* it got bad. Labor couldn't be too awful, or women wouldn't keep going through it and coming out with a smile. Positive thoughts. She would concentrate on positive thoughts. Uncle Dex would be at home when he got the news about the birth of his great-nephew, and her labor would be quick and relatively free of discomfort. And easy. *Easy* was definitely a positive thought, too.

Loosey barked again. "Okay," Annie said to the dog. "So neither one of us knows for sure what having a baby is like. Doesn't mean it couldn't happen just the way I'm thinking it might, does it?"

The dog wasn't paying attention. She was standing, almost pointing like a bird dog, alert to the sound of a truck engine outside. Her leg had healed and the cast was gone. She'd filled out nicely, too, losing the gauntness she'd had at the beginning of October. Her coat, too, was, if not perfectly groomed, clean and shiny. Annie had learned to be grateful for small things in the past two months, and at the top of that list was Loosey, furry companion extraordinaire. Annie voted her Top Dog of '99 and was willing to fight anyone who tried to take the title away.

That is, she'd fight as long as she didn't have to get up off the couch to do it.

There was the sound of a car door closing, carried clear on the night air, then footsteps to the front door. Even before the knock came, Loosey was beside herself with excitement, and Annie felt her heartbeat quicken with the hope that, maybe…just maybe…

"I'm coming," she called to the door, and began the rather involved process of getting up. But before she got her feet under her, the door opened and Alex walked in. Her world shifted, spun and settled into perfect place. His smile was all the fire she needed on a winter's day, his presence the only gift she ever hoped to receive. She would have

thrown herself wildly into his arms at that very
second, but life at this stage of impending motherhood just wasn't that simple. Besides, Loosey
had gotten there first, and man and dog were greet-
ing each other enthusiastically. "Hello, Sundance," Annie said when she could wait no longer.
"You're a little late for Christmas."

His eyes glistened with the blue-hot flame of
home fires and regret as he closed the door and
took off his hat, his coat and gloves. He was wearing her favorite blue shirt, one she'd given him
some time ago, with faded, but good-looking
Wranglers. Annie thought it was a positive sign
that she even noticed what he wore and how good
he looked in it. Something else to be grateful for.
A sign that one day her body and her hormones
would be normal again. "I'm sorry I missed
Thanksgiving and Christmas," he said. "But you
can't know how happy I am that I didn't miss the
most important day in my life."

She swallowed hard, reminded her heart not to
be too quick to forget even if he'd been forgiven
long ago. "And that would be...my birthday?"

He made a face. "No, because I have missed
that a time or two."

"Only by hours, and who's counting?" She
watched him swallow hard, then he covered the
distance between them in two long strides. Falling
back into the arms of the sofa, Annie smiled when
he eyed her reclining form. "I'd offer to scoot over
and give you room to sit down, but it's not that
easy."

"Then we'll do it the hard way," he said and knelt on one knee next to her. "I'm gonna say this fast, Annie, before I lose my nerve, so listen closely 'cause I'm pretty sure I won't be able to do it again." He inhaled sharply. "I have loved you since you were a gawky, freckle-faced, red-headed kid with more grit and heart than I knew I'd ever possess. I wanted your love back then so much I was willing to tackle Jason Kettridge, the baddest kid in eighth grade, just to get you to notice me. I still feel that way about you, Annie. I know we have some issues. I know I've disappointed you more times that I want to know about. And I know this sounds dumber than a mule with a ruffled shirt, but I thought if I never made you any promises, I'd never be able to break one. I thought, in my own foolish way, that I was protecting you from getting hurt."

She reached out, stroked his dear, dear face with her palm. "You weren't kidding about doing this the hard way, were you?"

"I'll do it standing on my head with my nose in the corner, if that's what it takes to get another chance with you, Annie. I know I'm coming to you late and pretty much empty-handed, with nothing but my name and a heartful of tender feelings. I can't promise I won't ever miss another one of your birthdays, but I will promise with my whole heart that I'll love you more than anybody else ever could and I'll be here with you. It may not always be easy, Annie, but I swear I'll make it good."

She wanted to speak then, but Loosey interrupted by sticking her head over Alex's elbow and licking his chin. He let go of Annie's hand and scratched the dog behind her left ear. "I'm happy to see you, too, Loose," he said. "But I'm in the middle of a proposal here, if you don't mind."

"A proposal?" Annie's voice sounded like it wanted to spring straight out of her throat and dance around. "You're proposing?"

Alex frowned. "Well, why did you think I got down on my knee?"

"So you didn't have to stand over me while you talked? So I wouldn't get a crick in my neck looking up at you?"

"It's a proposal," he said. "And you don't have to tell me my timing's a little off. I know this would have been better if it'd come last spring, before Josie's wedding."

Annie considered. "I'm not sure there's a bad time for a marriage proposal." She frowned, too. "It is marriage you're proposing, isn't it?"

"Would you believe me if I said I had something indecent in mind?"

She laughed, her heart lighter than it had been for months. Years, maybe. Alex had to be her destiny. Why else would the fates ordain that just the sight of him was enough to warm her from the inside out? "I wouldn't believe that for a second, no." She followed his gaze to her most prominent physical feature. "Not that the size of my belly isn't pretty indecent, already. Are you positive you want to marry me, knowing I can look like this?"

When she lifted her eyes to meet his, her heart skipped a beat. His expression was gentle, loving and so tender it took her breath away. "Knowing you can look like this is only part of the attraction, Annie. I've run my life backward pretty much from the start. Taking the chip on my shoulder and using it as an excuse to do whatever I damned well pleased. Searching for dreams in faraway places when you were here all along. You were right. I wasn't ready to be a father nine months ago and I don't know how good I'll be at it. But I'm here and I'm not going anywhere again. Not without you and my boy. And I don't even care if the baby is rightfully mine or if he inherits big teeth and an interest in African architecture from some other guy. He'll be your son and that's enough to make me want to be his daddy. If the two of you will have me...for better or worse?"

"We will," Annie declared, leaning forward as best she could to throw her arms around his neck. "Oh, your son and his mother most definitely will."

"*My* son?"

She nodded, loving the light of pride that sparked in his eyes. "As if I'd have a son with anyone else."

His kiss was all she'd ever longed for, the only dream she'd ever dreamed, and it wasn't until it had ended that she realized what Alex must have sacrificed in order to deliver it. "Where's Koby?" she asked.

"He was in Denver this afternoon when I decided I was not going to miss the birth of my son. A friend of mine, another trainer, offered to trailer him to the S-J for me.''

''But what about the futurity? You're supposed to ride him in the final event tomorrow night.'' She stopped, almost afraid to ask. ''Did he lose in the preliminaries?''

''Are you kidding? He was winning in a walk.'' Alex lifted his shoulder in a no-big-deal shrug. ''I withdrew him from the competition. Being here for you and Sam just turned out to be more important.''

She couldn't believe he'd done that, couldn't believe he was here. For her. ''But you staked your future as a trainer on him.''

''Winning that event tomorrow would definitely have given my career a jumpstart and there's no question it would have helped me get the S-J's breeding program going sooner rather than later. But today it suddenly hit me like a ton of bricks—those things will happen, anyway. I'm already fairly well-known on the cutting horse circuit. The S-J has never had the kind of breeding stock I intend to have, but it has a solid-gold reputation in other areas of ranching, thanks to Matt. Success may be slower coming, Annie, but it'll come. The important thing is I'll be here at the very second our son takes his first breath. I nearly missed that moment, for all the wrong reasons. I nearly lost you, the love of my life, by trying so hard to prove I was a man who deserved loving. I know I don't deserve you, Annie. Or this baby we're having. But

I'm gonna be grateful for you both until my last breath.''

"Oh, Alex," she said, blinking back the sweet tears of a happy heart. "You deserve so much more than you want to believe. I'm sorry I didn't put enough faith in you. I should have. It was selfish of me to expect you to do all the giving. And if you honestly don't want to live here, I'll move with you. We're a family now.''

"Move?" He looked around the cozy living room. "After I've just got this place spiffed up? I don't think so."

Annie kissed him again. "I meant move to Texas or some other state. But if you're happy here, so am I. In fact, I'm so happy I might as well be rolling in it.''

"You'd never get up," he pointed out realistically. "But since we've decided to start our married life in this little house, what do you think about adding on a room or two, in case Sam doesn't like being an only child?''

"Sam had better get born first, before he goes insisting we build onto the house.''

Alex reached for her hand and helped her lever up from the depths of the sofa cushions. "I know you're probably wondering what I'm going to fix you for supper, but try to keep your mind on me for a few more minutes, okay?''

She smiled, loving his take-charge, responsible attitude. Was it new? Or had she only now noticed? "Pizza," she said. "We'll order pizza and eat it in bed.''

"You're not listening, Doc. We're going to walk—well, you can waddle, if you'd rather—out to this four-wheel-drive vehicle I rented at the airport and we're going to drive over to see Reverend Whitehead and find out what we have to do to get married tonight. Then we're—"

"No, we're not." Annie decided to make things easy. "Not tonight, anyway. You're going to run me a nice, warm bubble bath and then you're going to get in the tub with me. If you'll fit, that is. Then we're going to get into bed with the pizza you've ordered and talk about whether we want to name our son Samuel Hoyt Thatcher McIntyre or Hoyt Alexander McIntyre Thatcher."

Alex cupped her face in his hands and kissed her. "Trust me, woman. I have your best interests at heart. We'll stop for pizza on the way to the reverend's and we'll have that bubble bath once we find out exactly how soon we can pull off a wedding. And his name will be Samuel Sundance McIntyre or, if he prefers, just 'The Kid.'"

Annie smiled and deferred. "All right," she said. "If that's what you want, that's what we'll do."

But they didn't. They went to the hospital instead.

Epilogue

Annie was sorry she'd eaten that pizza yesterday.

She was sorry she'd been in labor almost thirty hours.

She was doubly sorry that she'd ever had sex.

Alex leaned over her and wiped her face. "How're you doing?" he whispered, helpfully.

She seized the opportunity and grabbed his ear. "This hurts," she told him. "Don't let anyone kid you. It hurts a lot."

"I'd trade places with you in a heartbeat if I could, Annie."

"Don't think I wouldn't let you, either." She sighed, catching her breath between the rolling contractions. "Where's Dr. Elizabeth? Can't she do something to hurry this baby along?"

"I think your doctor has her hands full. I haven't seen her in quite a while, come to think of it. Of course, we've got at least three women in labor right now. There may be more before the night's over. Last I heard, Dr. Dave had called old Doc Wilson in to help, and another doctor is supposed

to be on his way to Bison City from Sheridan."
Alex brushed the damp hair back from her temple
and smiled. "Anybody might think you McIntyre
women concocted this whole First Baby of Bison
City contest so you could all go right down to the
wire."

"Not me." Annie declared her intentions quite
firmly. "I'm having this baby as soon as—" Another contraction momentarily disabled her train of
thought, and the only way she got through it was
because Alex let her mutilate his hand in a lethal
grip. When it passed, he wiped her face again and
told her soothing things about tomorrow. Things
like it would all be over tomorrow, and tomorrow
she could have chocolate and pizza. Well, maybe
a bite of each. Since she'd be breast-feeding, she'd
want to be careful what she ate, of course.

"I can't wait until tomorrow," she interrupted
his litany. "I can't wait until some stupid clock
chimes midnight. I can't wait another minute for
this to be over, do you understand?"

He nodded, kept his hold on her hand. "I do,
sweetheart, I do. And believe me, I don't care if
this baby is the Millennium Baby or the last—I
mean first—baby to arrive."

There was a clatter outside in the hallway and
somebody yelled, "I think she's in labor!" But
when Alex would have gone to investigate, Annie
stopped him cold. "You're with me, Sundance,"
she said. "Even if the whole pregnant population
of Bison City goes into labor, you are not to leave
me for a second. Okay?"

"I've traveled the country waiting to hear you say those words, Annie." He leaned down and kissed her lightly on the forehead. "I'm here for the rest of my life."

"Alex?" Willie came to the door. "Somebody sent you a telegram. Want it?"

"Sure, I guess." But Annie had a clench on his hand, and she wasn't about to let go. "Uh," he told Willie. "Why don't you read it to me."

There was the rattle of paper, then Willie's voice. "Okay, it says, 'Kodiak Blue wins with me in saddle. Stop. What the hell. Stop. He deserved it. Stop. Benny.' That's it." Willie folded the paper. "Got it?"

"Oh, yeah." Alex's smile had to be wider than Texas.

Annie hadn't thought she'd ever smile again, but suddenly she couldn't stop. "I heard. Congratulations, Alex. You picked a winner in Koby."

"I'm the luckiest son-of-a-gun you ever want to meet. Now, let's you and I get serious about having this baby."

"You think I haven't been serious for the past million and a half hours?"

"Just a little humor, okay? I'm with you, Annie. Just a little while longer and you'll be holding our son."

Another contraction built and rippled over her with excruciating discomfort. "This is the last time I'm having a baby in a small-town hospital with limited resources," she said as she rode it out.

"Next time we're forgetting this natural childbirth stuff and stocking up on anesthetics, okay?"

"Okay," he agreed, then asked. "So you think we'll be doing this again next year? You know, just in case the millennium doesn't actually start until January 1, 2001?"

Too exhausted to sock him in the jaw as he surely deserved for that comment, Annie glanced at the clock: 11:48.

"Alex," she said, feeling the shift in her body.

"I'm here, Annie. Hold my hand."

"If he's still not here at midnight, promise you'll just shoot me."

Alex grinned and kissed her again. "I promise," he said. "Baby by midnight or we're outta here."

*This holiday season, dash to
the delivery room with*

HARLEQUIN®

A M E R I C A N ◆ R O M A N C E®

Delivery
Room
DADS

**The McIntyre brothers of Bison City, Wyoming,
have no idea they're about to become daddies—
until a little stork tells them to hustle down to
the delivery room!**

*Don't miss this exciting new series from three of
your favorite American Romance® authors!*

**October 1999
BABY BY MIDNIGHT?**
by Karen Toller Whittenburg (#794)

**November 1999
COUNTDOWN TO BABY**
by Muriel Jensen (#798)

**December 1999
BABY 2000**
by Judy Christenberry (#802)

Available wherever Harlequin books are sold.

HARLEQUIN®
Makes any time special ™

"This book is DYNAMITE!"
—Kristine Rolofson

"A riveting page turner..."
—Joan Elliott Pickart

"Enough twists and turns to keep everyone
guessing... What a ride!"
—Jule McBride

See what all your favorite authors
are talking about.

Coming October 1999 to a retail store near you.

 **HARLEQUIN®**
Makes any time special™

 WIN A DREAM

In celebration of Harlequin®'s golden anniversary

Enter to win a *dream!* You could win:

- A luxurious trip for two to *The Renaissance Cottonwoods Resort* in Scottsdale, Arizona, or
- A bouquet of flowers once a week for a year from **FTD**, or
- A $500 shopping spree, or
- A fabulous bath & body gift basket, including **K-tel's** *Candlelight and Romance* 5-CD set.

Look for **WIN A DREAM** flash on specially marked Harlequin® titles by Penny Jordan, Dallas Schulze, Anne Stuart and Kristine Rolofson in October 1999*.

 FTD

R **RENAISSANCE. COTTONWOODS RESORT** SCOTTSDALE, ARIZONA

 K-TEL

*No purchase necessary—for contest details send a self-addressed envelope to Harlequin Makes Any Time Special Contest, P.O. Box 9069, Buffalo, NY, 14269-9069 (include contest name on self-addressed envelope). Contest ends December 31, 1999. Open to U.S. and Canadian residents who are 18 or over. Void where prohibited.

PHMATS-GR

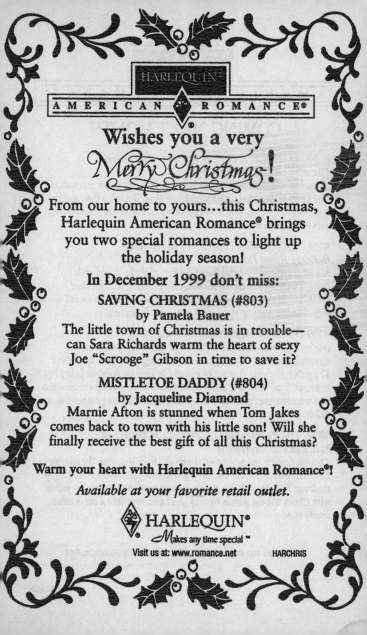

COMING NEXT MONTH

Look us up on-line at: http://www.romance.net